DOGBOY

|dogboy|

VICTOR KELLEHER

FRONT STREET
Asheville, North Carolina

Originally published by Penguin Group (Australia), 2005

Library of Congress Cataloging-in-Publication Data
Kelleher, Victor.
Dog boy / Victor Kelleher.—1st U.S. ed.
p. cm.
Summary: Given to the Great Father on the night of his birth,
Boy is reared by a dog in a village whose people barely tolerate
him, despite signs that he is favored, then travels far, striving to
find his rightful place in the brutal world of humans.
ISBN-13: 978-1-932425-76-5 (hardcover : alk. paper)
[1. Feral children—Fiction. 2. Self-esteem—Fiction. 3. Dogs—
Fiction. 4. Droughts—Fiction. 5. Rain and
rainfall—Fiction. 6. Villages—Fiction.] I. Title.
PZ7.K28127Dog 2006
[Fic]—dc22
2006000787

FRONT STREET
An Imprint of Boyds Mills Press, Inc.
A Highlights Company

815 Church Street
Honesdale, Pennsylvania 18431

DOGBOY

PART I

|the baby|

1

He was born on a bare hillside, near the end of what people called the "Dry Time."

No one else was present except his mother and a mongrel dog that trotted at her heels. Of the two, only the dog appeared pregnant. The woman's condition was hidden by a loose-fitting dress; and it was not until she gasped and clutched at the dress's loose folds that the swell of her belly became visible.

Beside her, the dog whimpered as she staggered to a halt, then let out a yelp of concern when she slumped to her knees in the raw dust.

The day was almost over. A mountain loomed through the fading light. Known as the Great Father, it stood taller than the surrounding peaks and blocked off this end of the valley.

An eagle, loosed from its aerie on the high crags, soared on silent wings. Wind gusted along powder-dry gullies, raising the dust in a soft mist. A distant bear rumbled a warning from its cavern home. And as the night settled on the lower valley, the woman groaned and went into labor.

For three hours she made no complaint, one hand clamped to her mouth to stop herself crying out. At last, with only the star-filled eyes of the dog as witness, she gave birth to a baby boy.

He lay squirming in the dust until she reached for him. Tired though she was, she coaxed the first gasping cry from his tiny body. The cord that bound him to her, she bit through with her teeth.

"Go free," she murmured.

He responded by groping blindly for her, but she took care to avoid his clutching hands.

"No, you are my gift to the mountain," she explained in a whisper. "To the Great Father. You are His to keep and care for."

Good as her word, she swaddled the child in a scrap of woolen cloth and eased him into a leather satchel she had brought. The satchel, with the child inside, she laid tenderly on the hillside.

Finally, she breathed a name into his ear: "Boy, I call you Boy." Then she left him there; abandoned him to the mountain and the mild spring night; gave him a final, tear-filled glance; and trudged off into the dark.

In her loose-fitting dress, she appeared unchanged from the woman who had arrived at this place hours earlier. Only the discarded satchel spoke of her recent ordeal and of the heartache that had replaced the child within her.

The dog, dutiful as ever, followed her into the night. At the limit of human earshot, however, it heard a cry and paused. Not so the woman. Deafened by grief, she stumbled on. The cry came again, a long wail of loss and longing. It was the kind of wail that only an infant can make, and the dog, caught between the child's grief and the woman's, lingered on the dark slope.

From overhead there came a peal of thunder, as though the mountain itself were answering the child's cries. A drop of rain brushed the dog's snout and landed between its front paws. More drops scarred the thick dust all around. Soon, the rain had grown to a downpour, great squalls sweeping across the lightning-slashed hillsides.

Farther up the valley, thunder rolled once more, like a voice from the mountain's heart, so loud that it almost dimmed the baby's cries. In a lightning flash, the dog glimpsed a wave shape gathering at the valley's head.

Was that what decided the dog to turn back? Or was it the rushing sound of a river in spate? Whatever the reason, it reached the child only minutes before the water descended. Tugging at the satchel's leather flap, it heaved the child farther up the slope. Higher and higher it went, its paws scrabbling in the dust, the crash of the river ever nearer.

The dog made its stand on a rough patch of rock, in the lee of a protective boulder. In the rain-thickened dark, a hissing wave surged past, its outer edges snatching at the satchel. Instantly, child and dog were swept along the bank, where by chance they lodged in a heap of ancient logs—the petrified remains of some long-forgotten forest.

There they lay, helpless, until the water receded hours later.

The mountain gave out a last rumble. The rain thinned and retreated. As a sliver of moon broke through the cloud, so the dog shook the river from its coat and settled its swollen body beside the now-sleeping child.

Near the end of that warm spring night the dog also went into labor. In a pool of pearl-gray light, three pups were born. Blind, mewing feebly, they reached for the nipple, and as they began to suckle, so too did the woken child.

That was more than the mother would tolerate. She turned and snapped, one of her teeth puncturing the lobe of the child's ear and leaving behind a jagged hole that wept bloody drops.

Too shocked to respond, the baby eyes stared blankly at

her. Straightaway she relented. After licking the wound clean, she lay back down and let the child continue feeding.

In the days that followed, the pups and child slept and fed together, sucking hungrily on the same milk-swollen teats, or lying in a tangle of warm limbs within the satchel.

The mother left them only at night, and then briefly, to hunt on the mountain's lower slopes.

It was a good time for wild game. Following the heavy rain, countless tiny rodents had emerged to feed on the fresh green shoots that pushed up through the once-parched soil. These scurrying creatures were easy prey for the dog, who usually filled her stomach within an hour.

After three days of such plenty, she began her return journey.

This took time and effort, because she was also burdened with the baby, regarded by now as one of her own. Much heavier than any pup, it weighed down the satchel and slowed her progress. With the satchel's flap gripped firmly between her teeth, she spent hours each day dragging her small family along the shoreline, her paws slithering in the mud.

The pups accepted the bumpy ride without complaint. So did the child. Although naked and filthy, he seemed content. Nestled among his doggy kin, he slept and woke according to their rhythms. He rarely cried. As if by instinct, he gave up human sounds and copied the pups' mewing call whenever he felt hungry. He even learned to growl softly to himself as he nuzzled the teat, or to whine in protest if the dog licked at the wound in his ear.

In this doglike state, and barely a week old, he was dragged to the edge of an upriver settlement.

A single hut, built of stone and clay, sat high above the

riverbank. It housed a ragged family of goatherders, people so poor that they owned nothing but their animals and the goatskin clothes they stood up in.

It was the aging wife who first came across the child. On her way to collect water, she glimpsed the satchel and the dog together, down on the muddy flats. When she approached, the satchel gave a twitch, and a blunt-muzzled pup crawled from the opening. Next, a tiny mud-streaked arm emerged—an unmistakably *human* arm—making her cry out in wonder.

Her cry brought the others running.

"What is it?" the goatherd demanded.

"A … a miracle," she said, and pointed at the child's waving arm.

The dog snarled a warning when the man ventured near, but he drove it off with a sweep of his stave.

"What have we here?" he demanded, and carelessly, one by one, he tossed the pups into the river.

While the mother swam frantically to save them, he groped for the child and held it up by one ankle.

"D'you call this a miracle?" he said with a laugh. "I call it one more mouth to feed, and we've too many of those already."

He was about to hurl the baby after the pups, when the wife bleated out a single word.

"Mercy!"

At the same instant, the bewildered child, as though recalling its human origins, began to wail bitterly.

Its outburst made the man hesitate … and in that brief pause, a growl of thunder sounded from the mountain. To the man's ears it came as a timely warning, and he snatched his hand away, letting the child fall into the mud.

"Did you hear?" he said in a whisper. "It's Him. The

Great Father. He's tellin' us to tread careful. Witchin' business, that's what this is, an' I'll have none of it. Nor will you," he told his wife. "Let the brat lie where it is. The river brought it to us, an' the river can take it away."

"But it's only a wee babe," she pleaded.

"So you say," the man snarled. "But I say it's half beast. Why else would it be in the care of that bitch there?"

She had no answer, and together with her silent children, she was ushered back to the hut.

The dog, meanwhile, had emerged from the pool, a live pup in her jaws. It was the only one she had managed to rescue. Gently she laid it beside the child, and then licked them both dry and clean. Yet her patient care failed for once to stop the child's whimpering. His recent fright had unsettled him, jolting him from his animal state.

The anxious dog tried offering the teat, but even that worked only for a while. With the milk fresh on his lips, he began to whimper again. As the day advanced, his distress grew into a series of abandoned cries that found echo in the far-off mountain.

Peal after peal of thunder issued from the heights. Black clouds rolled in along the valley, dimming the late afternoon light. And still the child wept, so loud and long that the woman disobeyed her husband and crept down through the falling dusk.

She took with her a makeshift crib—an open basket made from closely woven rushes. Also a stick for fending off the dog.

Snarling, it backed away. From a safe distance, it watched uneasily as she snuggled the child deep in the satchel, and then lodged the precious bundle in the crib.

"Sleep well, pretty boy," she murmured, and stole away, leaving him to the mercy of the moist night winds.

Soon after dark those winds brought more rain. Mutely, the woman listened to the squalls sweeping across the stone roof. She listened also to the baby's cries, which mounted higher as the storm increased.

Once, and only once, she peered out.

From up the valley there came a roar. In a flash of lightning she saw it—a solid wave of water—saw how it surged up the near bank, plucked the crib from where it lay, and rolled on.

Behind her the goatherd muttered gruffly: "It was neither man nor beast. Good riddance to it."

And she, in a dismal voice: "Lost …! Gone forever!"

The dog, however, was not so easily defeated. With the live pup clamped in her jaws, she had found safe purchase on higher ground. Now, she stared off into the gloom, noting the progress of the flood as it smashed a path along the valley floor.

She knew that somewhere in all that foaming water lay the child, and a muffled whine of longing broke from her throat. Her pup responded by wriggling feebly. She shook her head, signaling for it to be still. Then, tightening her hold on its tiny body, she set off at a gallop.

For some time she made steady progress downstream, always careful to match her pace to the speed of the flood. She never once thought to stop or rest. Her eyes fixed on the river's cresting wave, she followed it trustingly, on into the dark.

2

Her name was Magda, and she served the headman in the village of Bethel, a small upriver settlement. Once, the region around Bethel had been prosperous. But no more. Generations of drought had stripped away the topsoil in all but the deeps of the river valley, leaving behind a landscape of bony ridges and crags.

Bethel itself—perched above the riverbank and bounded on the landward side by a protective wall—consisted of a modest cluster of earth-and-reed huts. Although not much to look at, it was in fact more ancient than the great city of Delta, far downstream. Founded by a group of pioneer farmers, in the half-forgotten era of abundant rain, it owed its continued existence, in these less fortunate times, to the ruggedness of its people. And also to their faith in the eternal Spirit of the mountains, to whom they appealed whenever their crops failed and the parched land turned to stone. He, the Great Father, would always sustain them in the end, of that they were convinced.

Their simple faith, it seemed, had been rewarded yet again. For on this particular spring night, after a long and testing drought, Bethel lay bathed in healing rain. Throughout the village, people offered up their thanks and sank into untroubled sleep, lulled by the drift of rain against their thatched roofs.

Only a few remained wakeful—among them, Magda,

the serving woman. Hour after hour she tossed restlessly, conscious of the river roaring past, and of the distant murmur of thunder, high in the hills.

"Mercy ...," she breathed, each time the thunder rumbled through the night.

It ceased at last, and she fell into a fitful doze—though not for long. At the first hint of dawn, she was roused partly by the silence—for the rain had also stopped—and then by the yipping cry of a hound.

No longer very young, she sighed as she rose from her bed of dry reeds. She would have preferred to sleep on, because a day of labor lay ahead, but further rest was impossible with the dog barking like that.

What could be bothering the animal? Tying her hair in a loose knot, she stepped out into the cool of early morning.

She spotted the dog at once, down near the swollen river. It was dancing along the bank, barking excitedly at something in midstream.

Magda peered through the twilight, trying to make out what the thing could be. Some kind of container by the look of it. A reed basket, perhaps, it lay crushed against a rock, held there by the pressure of water.

"Fetch it," she instructed the dog.

Nervously, it ventured into the shallows, where the current knocked it off its feet. Only another line of rocks, farther downstream, prevented it from being swept away. Bedraggled and tired out, it floundered back to shore where it resumed its barking.

"Enough," Magda muttered, and silenced it with a click of the tongue.

Warily now, it watched as she lifted her long skirts and also ventured into the flood.

A few probing steps, the water riding above her knees,

and she was able to reach out and snatch the thing up. It felt strangely heavy, and moved when she placed it on the shore. Easing open the sodden neck of reeds, she revealed a stout leather satchel. And when she folded back the flap …!

She rose with a start, the color draining from her lips.

"What is it?" a voice demanded.

The headman—called Phylo—stood on the bank above her, his aging face almost as worn and leathery as the satchel.

"A … a child," she told him.

"Nonsense …!" he began, and stopped short as he also spied the child.

It lay fast asleep in its grubby woolen nest, unharmed except for an open wound in the lobe of one ear.

"Where did *this* come from?" he asked in astonishment.

Magda merely pointed to the river.

"You mean it's a … a gift from the Great Father?"

She answered now with a shrug, and he bent down in wonder, meaning to lift the child from its nest, but the dog leaped forward, teeth bared, and drove him back. Cursing, he picked up a fist-sized rock … and hesitated. For the dog had settled beside the child, which blinked awake and reached out hungrily. With a soft gurgle, it began to drink, its dimpled fists kneading the milk-swollen teat as if it were in fact a puppy.

Moments later an actual puppy crawled from beneath a shelf in the bank and also began to suck—the two bodies, one human, one animal, twined easily together.

Phylo spat in disgust.

"This is no child!" he declared. "No gift from the mountain. This is a beast in human form. Leave it be, that's my advice." He gave Magda a dark look and pointed skyward.

"The heavens will deal with it in their own way once the sun is high."

As he stomped off toward his hut, Magda glanced up at the dawn-pink sky. It was empty now, but she knew that within hours it would be dotted with hovering birds.

"What if the vultures peck out its eyes?" she called after him.

"That's for the heavens to fret about, not us," Phylo called back. "Now come away. The world of beasts is no concern of ours."

Out of long habit she obeyed, though her footsteps dragged on the upward slope; and in the course of her morning's work she stopped more than once to check on the small bundle down near the water's edge.

Gradually the heat of the day built up. Columns of hot air rose from the baking rocks, and with the mounting heat came the vultures, weighty birds, hook-beaked and watchful, that spiraled ever higher.

By midday the sky was thick with them. So many that Magda began listening for the clatter of descending wings. Sick at heart, she checked the shoreline yet again—only to find it empty!

Had the river perhaps reclaimed the child? Could the vultures have carried it away? But then where was the pup? Or the satchel and the woven basket?

Baffled, she was about to go and search when she heard a growl almost at her feet. She turned, and there was the dog, crouched in the shadow of the hut. It had dragged the basket up the slope and stowed it beneath the hut's eaves. Inside lay the child and the puppy, both fast asleep.

The dog growled again, as if to say, "Keep off," and Magda smiled to herself. What was it Phylo had said of the child earlier? *The heavens will deal with it in their own way.*

Yes, those had been his very words, and her smile broadened as she went busily about her work.

Phylo had a lot more to say later in the day. Both to her and to the other villagers who came to examine this strange dogboy.

"The child has damned itself with its unnatural ways," he announced grandly.

"Why is that?"

The question came from a man called Bartiss. He had once served as the village shaman, but had given up the role during the last long drought, after failing to coax rain from the clouds that hovered near the mountain.

"Just look at the child," Phylo answered reasonably. "It has turned to a dog for comfort. What decent woman would breast-feed it after this?" He shuddered at the idea. "No, it has sealed its doom. A week or two with only dog's milk to drink and it will fade away."

Ever ready to contradict him, Phylo's wife, Nessa, gave a short laugh.

"The child looks healthy enough to me. It had better get a move on if it means to die within the fortnight."

"Oh, it will die, all right," Phylo assured her. "No man can thrive as a beast, nor any beast as a man. The two are as different as … as earth and water. Mix them, and all you get is mud. Filth."

"Aye," Bartiss joined in, "the Great Father would never look kindly on a creature like this."

"Then why didn't the child die last night?" Magda asked quietly. "And how did it survive the flood?"

"Hold your tongue, woman," Nessa broke in sharply. "It's not for you to question your betters."

"No, Magda has a point, and she deserves an answer," Phylo said with a show of fairness. "As I see it, all things have a dark side. The day gives way to night, the sun to the moon, and birth to death. So it is with the Great Father's gift of rain, for it is followed by this mud-child. He is the night side of our good fortune; the curse to our blessing."

Phylo leaned back, more than satisfied by the nods of approval that greeted his account.

Only Magda seemed troubled by it.

"Forgive me, Master," she said humbly, "but I don't understand. A curse is one thing, a blessing another. How can they grow from each other?"

"Magda!" Nessa warned in a low voice.

Phylo placed a calming hand on his wife's shoulder. "This is a free village," he reminded her. "Even a landless servant has the right to speak her mind." Then more firmly to Magda: "Listen to me, woman, and learn. All good carries evil in its wake. That's the way of things. The rain falls and we enter a time of plenty; but with that plenty comes a plague of rats and mice. Well, it's the same with the river down there. Twice it has flooded in the past week, after years of drought. The first flood filled the riverbed to overflowing. The second brought us this ... this *half-beast*." He gestured toward the child who slept on, one arm curved around the pup. "Look at it! It's a crime against nature. Can't you see that?"

"If the child is a cursed thing, maybe we should finish it now," Bartiss suggested, fingering the dagger at his belt.

Close beside the sleeping child, the dog tensed. Its hackles rose, and it let out a soft growl.

"Hush," Magda breathed, but no one paid her or the dog any heed. They were too busy watching Phylo and Bartiss, the whole village aware of the rivalry between them.

"Use the knife if you will," Phylo told Bartiss in his grandest manner. "But remember this. The child is half-human as well as half-beast. So taking its life will make you half a murderer. Are you prepared to live with that?"

Bartiss considered the prospect, and then lowered his eyes as something stirred inside him—a long-held belief that the power of life and death belonged only to the Great Father.

"I'm no murderer, as you know full well," he muttered resentfully. "I was thinking of the village, that's all. Of how we'll all fare if we harbor a cursed creature here in our midst."

"We won't be harboring it for long," Phylo said confidently. "Leave it alone, and it will die of its own accord, like any neglected child."

"Only if we withhold its name," a voice rasped out.

Phylo's ancient mother had joined the gathering, her frail body supported by a cane.

"What's this about a name?" someone asked.

The old woman moistened thin lips. "You all know me as Sarah. It's who I am. Like the rest of you, I live through my name, and so does a baby. Once named, it becomes part of the human family and can claim a place among us. Deny it a name, and there is nowhere for its soul to lodge. It remains a shadowy thing, and must soon wither away."

"Then this child will have no name," Phylo decided. "He will be known as the dogboy, nothing else."

The gathering broke up after that, and for the rest of the day people gave the child a wide berth. Even Magda. She remained conscious of the child, though. Of its gurgling voice; of its waving hands and feet; of its puppyish whimpers whenever it felt hungry. And once, seeing the dog-mother trot over and lick its upturned face, she felt a pang of envy.

With the coming of night, she found its presence even

harder to ignore. Lying on her reed bed, with only the thickness of the hut wall between them, she was kept awake by its secret baby laughter. The sweetest of sounds, it seeped through cracks in the wall like a trickle of clear water.

It seemed to her a fitting noise for him to make—that clear-water sound—for he was after all a child of the river. And that meant he had to be blessed, surely, never mind what Phylo or Bartiss said. Didn't the mountain waters wash all things clean? Purify them? So whatever the child's faults—whatever the sins of his parents—they would have been washed away by now. No one could ride the river wave and emerge unchanged, unpurified.

Heartened by that thought, she rose and crept outside.

There was no sign of the guardian bitch, who was off somewhere hunting. As for the pup, it had crawled over to the ring of firestones and curled up in the warm ashes. Only the child remained wakeful. Secure in his wool and leather nest, he cooed happily, both hands groping upward, reaching for the half-moon that hung above the mountain.

With the moon behind her, Magda followed her own shadow around the hut to where the child lay. When she knelt beside him, blocking the moonlight, he blinked and reached for her face instead, the touch of his fingers making her heart contract with longing.

Something curious about those groping hands caught her eye. One was open, the fingers moving freely; the other stayed tightly closed, bunched into a fist. She pried the fist open tenderly, to reveal a small white pebble.

It was the kind of pebble found only in the depths of the riverbed, where water and sand polished the stones to a perfect smoothness. She gazed at it in astonishment. For this child to possess such a stone, he must have been down there in all that churning chaos! Rolled over and over far beneath the surface! How could he have survived the ordeal? Or managed to pluck this pure white pebble from the dark?

The same baby hand closed on the stone once more, as if for comfort, and Magda leaned nearer. Her puckered lips brushed across the rounded cheek.

"What a clever dogboy you are," she murmured, using the non-name Phylo had insisted on.

She noticed something else as she drew back: fresh blood, black in the moonlight, still leaked from the gash in his ear. The wound looked too jagged and raw to heal unaided. To close and scab over, it would need help of some kind.

On a string around her neck, she wore a single bear's tooth. Pulling it free, she slipped the tooth from the string. Smooth and sharp, whiter even than the pebble, it fitted the wound exactly.

There was a pained gasp as the tooth slid home. Magda fully expected the child to burst into tears, but his face cleared within moments; his eyes grew silver-bright as he glimpsed the moon across Magda's stooping shoulders. Gurgling happily, he stretched upward, his fingers again clutching at the pale disc.

"Yes, that's the way, dogboy," Magda breathed, her lips close to his ear. "Wish for the moon. For the moon and nothing less. Always."

3

He didn't weaken and die. On a steady diet of dog's milk, he flourished. His cheeks took on a ruddy glow, and his limbs grew brown and sturdy in the summer sun. Though like any other human baby, he remained helpless. Weeks passed, and still he was unable to crawl.

The puppy, on the other hand, spent her days romping in the dust. Forever curious, she explored every corner of the village, and chewed on anything she found. Puzzled by the dogboy's helplessness, she would growl and tug at his hair until he bleated for mercy; or nuzzle him roughly from his satchel home and leave him squirming on the hard ground.

Once, she dragged him close to the fire, where a stray spark landed in his woolen blanket. The smell of burning frightened the puppy away but brought the mother at a run. It brought Magda too. Between them they pulled him clear and doused the flames, which had already seared the skin across his back.

The dog licked at the raw wound for days afterwards, and within a week it began to heal. Curiously, the remaining scar looked very like a flame, as if the fire had marked him as its own.

"Unnatural," was the verdict of the villagers.

To them, the flame-shaped scar was further proof that this child was less than human. As they saw it, fire and water were natural enemies, and no normal child could be born of them both. Yet that was surely what had happened here. The dogboy had magically survived the flood, a river pebble clutched in one hand; and now he had emerged from the flames.

To make matters worse, someone attached the pebble to a leather thong and hung it around the child's neck, as a sort of talisman; a water sign to match the fire mark on his back. Who had been foolish enough to do such a thing? Didn't they realize there were forces at work here that were better left alone? No good would come of such meddling. Or so most of the villagers believed, and so Phylo continually reminded them.

"Don't be tempted by the human side of this child," he advised. "He is a dogboy, remember. Take the boy to your heart, and you take the beast also."

Bartiss, not to be outdone, added a warning of his own. "Those who show the child pity are traitors," he declared loudly. "They are opening us to … to …" He fluttered a hand vaguely, suggesting nameless evils that had yet to be revealed.

Despite his vagueness, most people took his warning seriously. So far they had merely ignored the dogboy. Now, when they ventured near, they averted their eyes and looked to the holy mountain instead: to the Great Father, the source of all good and natural things.

Yet months passed, and still the child flourished, thanks mainly to the dog. As her own pup matured, she devoted more time to his human needs. It was she who licked him clean every day; she who protected him from the night winds and falling dew; she who stood guard while he slept.

She could not protect him constantly, however. Hunger sometimes drove her off to hunt, and it was during one of these hunting trips, the dogboy barely six months old, that danger struck.

Magda was sweeping around Phylo's hut when it happened. In the hazy light of an autumn afternoon—the hills already purple with shadow—she heard a scream from overhead. Startled, she glanced up, in time to see a great feathered thing plummet from the sky.

It was one of the golden eagles that nested on the heights. Landing on the open satchel, it clamped its taloned feet around the baby head and surged upward—the child answering its bird cry with a scream of his own.

By then Magda had scurried across the clearing. With her broom she knocked the bird down and tried to grab the child, but was buffeted to her knees by the giant wings. Before she could rise, the bird was off again, lifting free of the ground and dragging the child with it.

A few more wing beats brought them to the edge of the village, nearly high enough to clear the enclosing wall. Of all the villagers, Magda alone gave chase, but fell farther behind at every stride.

"Stop them!" she sobbed—knowing in advance that no one would rush to help, least of all Bartiss, who stood off to one side, a foolish grin on his face.

In desperation she paused to scrabble for rocks on the hard-packed ground; found none, and looked up tearfully as the child let out another scream.

The eagle responded with a mighty flexing of the wings that carried it skyward. Already it was beyond human reach, though not quite high enough to elude the dog. Alerted by the child's screams, she came charging down the slope, used the village wall as a launching pad, and met the bird in midair.

Magda heard the impact of their bodies, then let out a small gasp of hope as all three—eagle, child, and dog—

crashed to the ground and rolled over and over in the dust.

The child was the first to break free. His face torn and bloodied, he lay whimpering against the wall. While Magda ran to snatch him up, the dog continued to attack. Its muzzle badly clawed, it worried at the bird, snapping mouthfuls of feathers that fluttered down around them.

The eagle backed away under the onslaught. A single ungainly hop took it to the top of the wall. There it stood at bay, ruffled and defiant, screeching out a protest. Then it gave another hop and was airborne, as its spread wings caught an upward draft.

Satisfied, the dog trotted over and nosed at the quivering child, now clutched in Magda's arms.

"Don't worry," she told the animal. "He's all right with me."

In fact, she knew the child was far from all right. She could feel his heart hammering wildly; feel his warm blood soaking through her dress. And why didn't he cry? He gave a soft whimper, that was all, which the mountain seemed to answer. But it was just autumn thunder, faint and distant, the clouds around the high peak lit from within.

Holding the child tenderly, she returned to the hut where she saw to his injuries. Only one was serious: a jagged cut, left by the bird's talons, which ran from the corner of his eye, up across the brow. Between the wound's rough edges, the white of his skull showed through; and the eye where the cut began was filled with blood.

"Poor boy," Magda sighed, convinced that he was half blind. "You had so little to begin with. Now this." And she smiled tearfully down at him.

To her amazement, his bloodied face suddenly crinkled up and he smiled back—his very first smile, as if he had only now discovered his human side.

"You are a miracle!" Magda whispered, and pressed him briefly to her breast.

Then, having stemmed the flow of blood as best she could, she placed him back in his weathered satchel, where the dog fed him and added her care to Magda's, by licking lovingly at his wounds.

By nightfall, curled up between the dog's paws, he was again gurgling softly to himself, as though nothing had occurred. Somewhere—in the folds of his blanket perhaps—he had found a new toy: an eagle feather, which he passed from hand to hand and smiled at happily, like any normal child.

Seeing the feather clutched in his tiny fist, Magda felt her heart lurch in wonder. Was this yet another sign, like the pebble and the flame-shaped scar? Proof that he was a child not just of fire and water, but also of the sky—of the air she breathed?

She could not doubt it. Squatting beside him, she eased the feather from his grasp and looped it onto the same string that held the pebble. There it lay against his baby skin, like a flash of gold in the fading twilight.

"Sleep well, dogboy," she murmured.

He slept surprisingly well in the nights that followed, untroubled by his ordeal. Untroubled, too, by his damaged eye and ugly head wound. The eye healed quickly, and despite Magda's fears, he suffered no loss of sight. As for the head wound, it formed a dark scab, which gradually flaked away, leaving behind a claw-shaped scar. The sight of the scar made the villagers ever more wary of him, but he continued to flourish just the same.

Soon, like any other child his age, he began to teethe. Hearing his small whimpers of distress, Magda crept out in the night and gave him a dry root to chew on; but by morning he had discarded it in favor of a fresh bone brought by the dog. This he fought over with the half-grown puppy, hanging on so grimly that the puppy finally gave up and left him gnawing on the shreds of meat and gristle that were still attached to the bone.

The dog brought many more bones after that, and even hunks of raw meat, which he sucked at until they were soft enough to swallow. He was nearly nine months old now, crawling around the village and learning to stand—which surprised the villagers who had believed he would never walk like a human.

He proved them wrong by midwinter. Magda emerged early one morning—the air sharp with frost—and noticed baby footmarks on the frosted ground. She followed them around the hut, and there he was, staggering across the sun-bright clearing, the dog at his side, one hand clenched onto the dog's ear for balance.

Nobody praised his efforts.

"For shame," the villagers complained. "A child of that age should be decently covered."

"Aye," Bartiss joined in. "Only a dogboy would parade his nakedness."

For once, Magda agreed, and by the next morning he was wearing a leather apron that reached to his knees. Unfortunately, the puppy took a liking to it, and chewed most of it away, but a narrow strip remained—enough of a covering to satisfy the village.

The winter brought more than cold to the dogboy, however. More even than the human gift of walking upright. It also brought a marauding bear, driven down from the mountain in search of food. By rights the creature should have been sleeping in some distant cave, but something had raised it from its winter torpor: some strange impulse that made people like Phylo ponder the mystery of it for weeks to come.

"It must have been the child's dog-spirit that woke the animal," he told anyone who would listen. "For it's the child's presence that lured it down here. You saw them, how they approached each other, as beast to beast. How the bear had eyes for none but the dogboy."

Old Sarah could never resist adding her opinion: "You're right there, my son. The child and the bear are animal kin. Why else would the bear have singled him out? Bears, as we know, cannot abide a rival. If you ask me, it came here for the sole purpose of quenching his spirit. For all we know, the Great Father Himself may have sent it to relieve us of the child."

"Good riddance to the brat, I say," Bartiss muttered in the background.

But all of this came after the event, of course, and after the mangled body of the dogboy had been cast out.

The event itself was far more dramatic. It occurred toward the end of winter, when the dogboy was nearly one year old, and on a day made chill by a sharp wind that swept down from the mountain.

It began with a loud crash and a roar that brought people running from their huts or in from the neighboring gardens. What they discovered was a hole in the western wall of the village and, standing in the gap, the shaggy form of a mountain bear. Still covered in dust from the fallen wall, it reared up at the sight of them and roared a challenge. Most people had sense enough to run, but a few took refuge in their huts or grabbed brands from the fires, for defense. Only one villager showed no fear at all—the dogboy.

Perhaps if his dog-mother had been present, he might also have run off, but she was hunting on the mountain with her female pup. Alone and undefended, he staggered *toward* the noise, not away from it, drawn on by curiosity. The bear, which he glimpsed between the huts, did not alarm him. To his baby eyes, the creature looked like some monstrous toy—a new and exciting thing for him to play with—and letting out a ripple of laughter, he moved forward, both arms outstretched.

Who can say what the bear saw in the child? Or whether it noticed him at all in those first moments? Sniffing the air, it caught a whiff of food from the cooking fires, and lurched into a run. The child, as it happened, lay directly in its way, his arms spread wide in welcome; and the bear swatted at him with one huge paw. Probably, it wanted only to clear a path to the food, but the longest of its claws punctured the baby heel and lodged there.

Maddened by this squirming thing which seemed to cling on, the bear stopped and shook its paw, the child's body jiggling helplessly. That only maddened the animal further, which rocked backwards, right onto one of the cooking fires!

The heat and the stench of its own singed fur made it roar in protest. With its free paw, it turned and swatted at the fire, and was burned again for its trouble. Here was a very real enemy, one it knew and understood, for it had caught the tang of brush fires on the mountain often enough, after lightning strikes. It had even run from one in its younger days.

The memory of its youthful terror came back to it now, and it galloped back across the village, the child's forgotten body dragging in the dust. It might easily have dragged the child right up to the heights, and devoured it there; but as it leaped through the gap in the village wall, the body caught in the rubble and pulled clear, the bear's claw still lodged in its heel.

That was where the villagers found the dogboy minutes later, half buried by fallen stones and clay.

Old Sarah turned the damaged body over and examined it briefly.

"Dead," she pronounced.

Magda, beside herself with grief, tried to scoop the child up, but Phylo held her back.

"You would not follow the departed beast to its lair," he cautioned her. "Nor should you pursue this animal spirit beyond the grave, because it too will consume you."

The disposal of the body was left to Nessa, who treated it as she would any other dead animal. Slipping it into its satchel, she took it to the northern edge of the village, where the wall was highest, and threw it over into the dry wilderness of rocks that lay beyond.

She heard it land with a soft thud.

"That's the end of witchery," she murmured, dusting her hands clean.

4

By day, Magda went about her work as usual. She had no choice: she was landless, poor, and dependent on others. In her youth, like all women of the village, she had wished for marriage, land, children—for a son especially, to support her in her declining years. Yet all her hopes had come to nothing. And so now, at night, when the rest of the village slept, she alone mourned for the passing of the dogboy, as though grieving for a lost son.

One night, toward the end of winter, she could stifle her tears no longer. Slipping from her rush bed, she padded out into the dark. It was an hour or two from dawn, a half moon hovering above the mountain. There was no wind, and the air, although chill, was free of frost.

Through the stillness, she could hear the high yip-yip-yip of a young dog. She listened hard, trying to interpret the sound. The animal was clearly calling to someone or something, but whether in distress or joy she could not decide.

As the cries rose higher, she followed them, threading her way between the moonlit huts. She could tell now that the sound was coming from outside the village, and she almost turned back. There were wild dogs in plenty on the mountain, animals that had strayed from the village in years gone by, never to return, and she knew the danger of encountering them at night. Except that what she could hear was a young dog—too young by far to be running with a pack—and it was that thought which drew her on.

She reached the village wall in the last of the moonlight. The wall was high at this point, built with large boulders from the river. Feeling for hand- and footholds, she climbed up and peered over. Yes! As she had first feared, a pack of wild dogs stood ranged across the hillside; and they had the look of dogs on the hunt, for they were picking their way warily down the slope, their ears held flat, their tails low.

By rights, the young animal below—too close to the wall for Magda to see—should have been calling out in fear. Yet there was an excitement to its cries, a joy perhaps, which puzzled her.

Curious, she climbed higher and looked down ... at the dogboy! He was sitting upright in his satchel, both baby arms waving at the advancing dogs.

Magda had grown up in this desert valley. She understood how, in the heat of the day, it could play tricks with the eyes: reveal pools of cool water to the thirsty or groves of date palms to the hungry. But such things could not happen at night! Surely!

Magda rubbed her eyes in amazement, half expecting the child to disappear; to dissolve back into the earth that had claimed it weeks earlier. Hardly daring to hope, she looked again. Nothing had changed. This was no desert mirage, no cruel trick played on her by the night spirits, but a flesh-and-blood child who had somehow survived yet another ordeal. The most testing of them all: the gates of death.

A true miracle! That was her first thought, and she offered up a silent prayer to the Great Father. For His bounty. For this blessing. She did not rush her prayer. It was too important for that. A full minute passed before she raised her head, and by then the child had crawled from the satchel and begun tottering up the slope to meet the pack.

She heard his breathy chuckle, his cooing laughter, even as she leaped down from the wall. Three strides, and she had the dogboy by the hair, lifting him clear of the lead hound that lunged and snapped. She tried to kick it away, and felt its fangs slice across her ankle. She screamed out then, in anger more than pain, and as the pack held back for a moment, she tucked the child safely under her arm and groped for rocks with her free hand. That also made the pack pause—long enough for her to turn and leap for the wall.

The pack followed, as she knew they would. She felt them pulling at the hem of her shift; felt their teeth graze both calves; and then she was out of reach, already sliding down the inner face of the wall.

The commotion had roused most of the village. Armed with whatever was at hand, they came running from their huts. Someone had brought a lamp, which was thrust into her face.

"What is it?" Phylo's voice demanded. "What's going on here?"

Her answer was to show him the dogboy, this miracle of the night.

There was a nervous silence.

"Is it real?" someone breathed.

"As real as you and me," she told them, and pointed to the bear's claw, still lodged in the child's heel.

"But it was dead," Nessa protested. "I cast its body out myself."

"Can the bear destroy what the fire and the water have spared?" Magda countered.

"The bear is a lord of the earth," Bartiss broke in. "It answers to no one but itself."

"Aye, and the eagle is a monarch of the skies, but still the child prevailed against it."

Some of the villagers nodded in agreement, prompting old Sarah to side with Magda.

"There's a mystery at work here," she said slowly. "Perhaps the dogboy belongs on the hillside with its own wild kin. Perhaps not. I say we take the child back until the Great Father reveals its fate."

Phylo stepped forward into the light. "These are wise words," he announced importantly. "We would be foolish to banish a creature that the elements have spared. We must make room for him here in the village."

Nobody disagreed, not even Bartiss, and there the matter would have ended but for the mother dog, who chose that moment to return from her nightly hunt.

She announced her return with a scrabble of claws and a throaty growl. Someone lifted the light high, and there she stood atop the wall, the mangled body of a hare clamped in her jaws. Leaping down, she offered her kill to the dogboy, who reached for it hungrily and began tearing at the carcass with his baby teeth.

That was too much for the villagers. And for Magda too, who let the child slide from her arms, down into the dust.

"Is *this* what you want us to take into our homes?" someone shouted. "*This?*"

"Yes, cast it out!" others added. "It's no better than a wild beast."

Bartiss advanced on the child, meaning to hurl it over the wall, but already the dog had moved to its side. A snap and a growl sent Bartiss scurrying backwards. Several shrill barks warned off anyone else foolish enough to challenge her.

The child, meanwhile, continued to feed on the raw carcass, its hands and face now covered in gore.

"Phaugh!" people exclaimed in disgust, and turned toward their huts.

Phylo and Magda were the last to leave.

"For the present, we'll let it bide here by the wall," Phylo instructed her. "But I'll not have it come any closer, d'you hear? So don't go enticing it with tidbits and kind words, or you'll find yourself sharing the bare hillside out there."

Despite his instructions, Magda could not resist checking on the child soon after daybreak. By then, the dog had licked it clean and it lay curled up in the dust, its head resting on her belly.

The dog growled at Magda's approach; and again when Magda returned from the far side of the wall, satchel in hand.

"For him," Magda murmured, as though speaking to a fellow human, and placed the open satchel on the ground. With the dog looking on warily, she slid the sleeping child inside.

The dogboy did not wake. Not even when, on impulse, Magda plucked the bear's claw from its heel. It merely whimpered, causing the dog to mouth Magda's wrist warningly.

"Easy ... easy ...," she breathed, and looped the claw onto the string around the child's neck, adding it to the feather and the stone.

Lovingly, she brought her lips close. "Guard these things well, dogboy," she whispered. "They are your protection. Your blessing."

5

At first, no villagers would tolerate the dogboy among the huts. Whenever he wandered over, they would wave sticks in his face and drive him away. He did not go willingly. Nor did he seem frightened. Often, all their shouting and stick waving produced little more than childish laughter. Minutes later he would be back, peering in through their hut doors, watching curiously as they went about their daily tasks.

The lighting of the fires in the early morning, the preparation of oatcakes and herbal teas, the mending and weaving of woolen cloth—these and other tasks held his attention for hours on end. With his head cocked to one side, his eyes alive with interest, he would take in the villagers' every move, as if committing their many skills to memory.

For their part, the villagers soon grew tired of driving him off. What was the point? He did them no harm. As the weeks lengthened into months, most people learned to accept his presence. And even the most hardhearted of them had to admit he was an endearing child; surprisingly intelligent for a beast, and with a ready smile on his face.

Yet still nobody fed him. The dog did that. Nightly, she brought fresh meat from the mountain—rodents, rabbits, small birds, whatever she could find. He accepted her offerings readily. Too readily, the villagers maintained. For it was the sight of him wandering past their doors, his face bloodied from his recent meal, that persuaded them to go on rejecting him. After all, how could anyone take to their hearts a beast—never mind how human he looked—a wild creature, half boy, half dog, who wolfed down his food raw? Here was the proof of his true nature; proof that he deserved no place in the vast and sprawling family of humankind.

He would never learn to speak, for instance. Of that they were certain. His whimpers and growls, like his relish for raw flesh, marked him out for the animal kingdom. It was a kingdom that would reclaim him eventually—they were certain of that too. In the meantime, they tolerated his presence; smiled at his antics when he wrestled with the other dogs in the dust; joined in his laughter as it echoed through the village.

Of course, he did not always laugh. That was something else they noticed. There were times when he was pensive, preoccupied with thoughts of his own.

"Dog-thoughts, that's all he's capable of," Bartiss was fond of announcing. "I've seen him up there on the wall at night, on the lookout for wild dogs. They're all he's really interested in. All he has eyes for."

Bartiss wasn't exaggerating. The dogboy *did* spend a good deal of time looking for wild packs. They fascinated him. Early and late, he climbed the wall in the hope of sighting them, and his howling cries would announce their arrival.

"There he goes, calling to his kin," the villagers would say, and nod knowingly. "One of these days he'll run off with the pack, you'll see."

But more months passed, and still he showed no inclination to wander off. He seemed content to dwell at the edge of village life, which he found just as fascinating as the wild dogs.

In the early evening, he liked nothing better than to

creep close to one of the cooking fires and listen to the village talk: to the current gossip and the retelling of old stories; to the songs of more heroic times; or to the low chants and lilting melodies that centered always on their faith in the kindness of the Great Father. How much of this he understood, nobody could say. As with his watchfulness earlier in the day, he always listened in silence. Except for occasional outbursts of impish laughter, no human sound escaped his lips.

"He's lonely, that's why he comes to us," Phylo declared. "For that, and no other reason."

And most people agreed.

They might have had doubts, however, had they observed him later in the evening, after the village had retired to bed. Then, his face lit by the lingering fire glow, he would make strange, half-strangled sounds deep in his throat, as if struggling to release the human self trapped within.

It was much the same when he went down to the river to drink. Crouched on the bank, his face close to the water, he could be seen muttering softly to himself. Or was it perhaps the river he was addressing? His voice as murmurous as the passing wind.

"Bewitched, that's what he is," Nessa insisted, convinced that she'd been right all along. "If we had any sense, we'd give him back to the wild."

"But he doesn't belong out there," Magda argued desperately. "You saw how the bear and the eagle tried to claim him, and they both failed."

"Hush, woman," Phylo told her. "Nessa's right. The boy's an odd one. We keep him here at our peril, if truth be told."

Although most people agreed, no one went so far as to banish the child. He had been with them three years now and had become a kind of habit. They had grown used to his sturdy little frame toddling about the village. Had he vanished suddenly, they would almost have missed him.

And so, despite their distrust, more seasons slipped by, the boy growing taller by the month.

As a five-year-old, he remained filthy and unkempt, and he still lacked the strength to hunt with the mother dog on the mountain. Yet from his observation of the villagers, he had acquired a surprising number of skills. Like them, he could make fire using nothing but two sticks, a length of grass string, and a heap of dry moss or leaves. Similarly, he knew how to scrape and cure the skins stripped from rabbit carcasses; and how to fashion those same skins into a crudely stitched blanket, for warmth on chilly nights. To add to his comfort, he had learned the rudiments of weaving, and made for himself a lop-sided length of rush matting.

Far more mysterious, however, were his less human skills: those he had somehow plucked from the untamed world of nature. Like a creature of the wild, he had the ability to read the skies: to foretell the coming of high wind or unusually hot weather. He also understood the ways of the earth. Big enough now to venture up into the foothills, he knew as if by instinct where to dig for edible roots, and usually came back with his satchel full.

These roots and tubers soon supplied about half his food. On a fire of his own making, over by the wall, he roasted them each evening. Magda, busy with her end-of-day tasks, would look across to the gleaming jewel of his fire, to where he and his sister hound—the pup who had shared his satchel—now shared a nightly feast.

One night more than any other stood out in her memory. It was early winter, the descending dusk sharp with frost.

Through the chill air she caught the scent of something more than roasted roots.

She hurried over, her work forgotten, convinced now that she could smell cooking meat. Sure enough, he had rigged a spit above the fire—the type used throughout the village—and was roasting a skinned rabbit. He offered her some, laughing; aware, in his childish way, of his own cleverness.

She felt real joy stir within her as she took the cooked meat from his hand. Relief too.

"Good boy," she murmured approvingly.

When she told the villagers of this, no one was impressed.

"He is aping the way of men, nothing else," Phylo said with a shrug. "All half-tame creatures do that to some degree."

As usual, Bartiss went one step further. "It's in the nature of dogs to learn a trick or two."

"But to *cook* …?" Magda objected.

"To herd, to cook, to run and fetch—what's the difference?" Nessa interrupted impatiently. "He's a dogboy still."

Had they learned of his other skill, they might have thought differently. But this he practiced far from the village, farther downstream, where the narrow, rock-strewn riverbed gave way to long sandy stretches.

Since the flood that had delivered him, there had been little rain. In his fifth and sixth years, this drought deepened, taking an iron grip on the mountains and the valleys below. The river was reduced to a trickle; then to random pools; and finally to a parched bed. To find water for their meager crops, the villagers had to dig down through layers of sand

and rock, and these wells, as the months passed, grew ever deeper.

Soon, water became more valuable than food. Each person received his or her daily portion, and not a drop more. The dogs and the dogboy, not being human, had to fend for themselves.

As old Sarah put it: "How can you favor a half-beast when your children's lips are cracked and dry?"

Not even Magda could dispute that, though her heart still went out to the dogboy. More than once, in the dead of night, she took him some of her own water, and was surprised when he refused it. She was equally surprised by his appearance—by his full-fleshed lips and cheeks. Unlike the other children in the village, he did not seem parched and dry, his skin wizened by the drought. Beneath the grime that covered him from head to toe, he had the look of someone who lived in a land of plenty.

"All the more reason to think him bewitched," was Nessa's verdict.

"Or akin to the wild things," Sarah suggested. "For it's only mountain creatures that flourish in these trying times."

The truth about the dogboy was far simpler. Early and late each day, he and his doggy sister loped off downriver, to where the sandy stretches began. There, they searched and sniffed until they caught the scent of water, and then set themselves to dig. A meter down, sometimes less, they would tap into a buried stream, fresh water gushing into their sandy hollows—more than enough to meet their daily needs.

Had the villagers asked him to, he would gladly have dug for them. Or at least shown them where best to sink their wells. But they never thought to look to him for advice; and he was a mere child, convinced that the mysterious world of humankind stood above him in all things.

There had been droughts before, but never like this one. Year by year, its grip tightened. By the time he turned seven, the village wells were thirty meters deep, and produced only a trickle of water. Nothing could be spared for the gardens now. In desperation, parties of hunters took to the mountains. But these were farming people, unskilled in the hunt, and they came home empty-handed. When their gardens also failed, they were reduced to gathering grasses and rose hips on the mountain slopes. At night, the children cried out in hunger.

The wild creatures were as desperate as the villagers. The bears grew thin and bad-tempered; the eagles screeched in protest; rodents and rabbits became a rarity. For the mother dog, as for everyone else, these were hard times. Night after night, she returned to the village with nothing to show for her hours of hunting. She, too, grew rib-thin. She looked now to the dogboy for help, wolfing down a portion of roasted roots each dawn.

It was not in her nature to give up, however, despite her failing strength. She continued to drive herself until the very end—which occurred one night toward the end of summer.

She had made a kill high in the rocky crags that fringed the peaks—snapping up one of the few remaining rabbits. Half the carcass she ate there and then. The other half, as always, she intended for the dogboy. As she mouthed the flesh and loped off along a nearby gully, she was confronted by the hunched figure of a bear. There was no going around the animal: the gully was too narrow, its sides too steep. Nor was there any question of abandoning her kill. Bear and dog eyed each other suspiciously; both growled defiance; both read the other's needs and charged.

There was only one possible outcome. The wonder of it

was that the dog escaped alive—though barely—and that she managed to retain her kill. Badly wounded, bleeding from an ugly wound that ran the length of her back, she limped off down the mountain.

She was close to death when she reached the village. In the first light of dawn, she had just enough strength to clamber across the wall and drop the kill at the dogboy's feet. That done, she rolled over and died.

He was alone when this happened. His sister pup was off on some foraging trip of her own, and Magda—always the first of the villagers to rise—had yet to emerge from her hut. Alone, desolate, with no one to turn to, he cradled the dead body in his arms and gave way to childlike grief.

He had not cried like this since those far-off days when his human mother had abandoned him. He had complained and whimpered often enough, as all children do. He had screamed in terror when the eagle and the bear took him, and when the fire licked across his back, leaving its mark on his baby flesh. But bitter tears like these, shed for another, not for himself, these were something new in his life. Like the choking sobs that racked his body, they were painful and hard to bear.

Throughout the morning, he cried alone. Or not quite alone perhaps, for Magda looked on with a grieving heart. Also, it had been many years since the last good rain. A break in the drought was long overdue. And now, as if in sympathy with his plight, thunder rumbled from the distant mountain; lightning, faint in the sunlight, flashed across its rock-dark peaks; heaped clouds swept in across the valley, their undersides dyed deepest black.

By late morning it had begun to rain. A light drizzle at first, it grew into a downpour, and then into a mighty storm that swept down from the heights and battered the tiny settlements along the valley. That night, the river began to flow again, soon swelling to a flood that matched the fury of the storm.

This was a rare time for the villagers, and called for joy, celebration. It was not a time to look to the needs of an unwanted waif called the dogboy. While he sobbed out his misery, the village people danced and sang. Except for Magda—a silent partner in his grief—they hardly noticed him over by the wall, washed clean at last by the ongoing downpour, the dead body of the dog draped across his lap.

Whole days passed before the rain stopped. And still the dogboy was the last thing on the villagers' minds. They had other worries, such as the building of a levee to keep the worst of the flood from their huts. Next, there were the abandoned gardens to be seen to; the stored seed to be planted in the wet soil; the flurry of weeds, which always followed hard upon rain, to be rooted out.

These tasks took further days, weeks; and while the villagers labored on, Magda was the only one among them who cast caring eyes in the dogboy's direction. She tried going to him, of course, but he pelted her with bones and drove her back. Still watchful, keeping her distance, she followed the passage of his grief—grieving for him in turn, but also curious.

What would he do now? That was the question that plagued and puzzled her. It also made her fear for him. The dog had been the only mother he knew. How would he cope without her?

He showed no signs of coping to begin with. Hour after hour, day after day, he sat in the rain, the dog cradled in his arms. When the body began to putrefy, he clung to it still. Magda, returning wearily to her hut, caught a whiff of dead flesh on the evening breeze, and she went to him again. She endured his barrage of bones; ignored the way he barked and snapped at her; felt for the first time the nip of his teeth on her bare flesh.

"Come," she murmured softly. "Give her up now. It's time."

He gazed tearfully into Magda's face, the scar on his brow twisted into a kind of question mark. Did he understand her words? He seemed to, because he shook his head.

Encouraged, Magda tried explaining the nature of death to him. "This animal—your mother—she has walked her path through life and reached the end," she said in a saddened whisper. "The earth has claimed her for itself and no one can bring her back. You must let her go, and allow her to sleep the long sleep of the dead."

Reluctantly, he released the body, though as Magda lifted it from his arms, he gave a howl of longing. Like a lost pup in a storm, he followed her, weeping, as she clambered over the wall; helped her build a cairn of stones on the open hillside.

Magda had planned to bury the animal beside the cairn, which would serve as a marker to the grave, but he would have none of that. The moment she began digging in the sodden earth, he shook his head for her to stop.

"What then …?" she asked.

Tenderly, he gathered up the body and deposited it on the very top of the cairn.

"But the vultures will get it there," she told him.

He mouthed the word in clumsy imitation: "Vut-ters."

Magda stepped back in astonishment. "Yes, scavenger birds," she added eagerly. "Like this." She flapped her arms and stretched out her neck.

Again he seemed to understand, because he nodded for

a second time and patted the dog's body to show it should remain there.

"Do you want them to eat it?" she asked, baffled by him.

And he mouthed his second word: "E-a-t ... e-a-t."

Did he truly grasp the word's meaning? There was no time for Magda to find out, because Phylo was calling from the village.

"Magda, you lazy wretch! Where are you?"

She left him in the teeming rain and returned to her work. In her heart, however, she remained at his side.

Pausing in her labors, she would glance across to where he sat, hunched and still, on the outer wall. He no longer wept—she was deeply grateful for that small mercy. His tears and the rain—or so it seemed to her—had stopped together. Soon, the clouds rolled away, and with the sunlight came the vultures.

She thought the birds would disturb his vigil and drive him back into the village. But when they descended with loud squawks and a flurry of wings, he held up his arms as if in welcome.

"Look at him!" Nessa said in disgust, and spat into the fire. "He knows his own kin when he sees them."

His "kin," as she called them, made short work of the dog's carcass. They picked it clean within hours, and left the larger bones strewn around the hillside, where, within a week, they bleached in the sunlight. Most of these he gathered up and deposited on the cairn, as a type of shrine. The largest of the remains, the skull, he kept for himself.

The first Magda knew of this was when he appeared before her some days later. As always, he wore the necklace she had fashioned for him, with its feather, stone, and claw. Now, though, he had made a second necklace, from strands of coarse grass twisted together. This one held a single object—the dog's whitened skull—the grass string threaded through its empty eye-sockets.

She gave a small cry of horror when she saw it.

"No!" she protested. "You mustn't wear this. It's wrong."

She reached for the necklace, meaning to snatch it free, but he caught at her wrist and held it firm. Pushing her hand gently away, he stabbed at the skull with one finger.

"Mo-oth-er ...," he began falteringly, and then stabbed at his own chest. "Me ... dog ... same."

She wasn't ready for this act of speech, though a moment's reflection told her where it had come from. Those many nights he had spent listening to the village talk, *they* surely had to be the source of this human awakening. Crouched in the firelight, he must have been learning as well as listening, like all the other village children. For clearly he understood not just the words themselves, but also how to order them into a pattern of meaning.

"You're a real boy!" she murmured, thrilled by her discovery. "You don't belong among the beasts. You never have."

But he disagreed. "Dog ...!" he insisted. "Only ... dog." And there was no ignoring the pride in his voice; the confident belief that he had at last fathomed his true identity.

Except he wasn't a dog! Magda felt certain of that now, never mind what Phylo and Bartiss and the rest of them said. Never mind even what the child himself had come to believe.

"No!" she protested for a second time, desperate to convince him. "You're human, like me. You can speak."

He shook his head, and when she looked into his eyes, she saw a change there. The dog's death had done something to him: he seemed older somehow, more knowing.

"Me ... not ... human," he cried, again stabbing at his chest. "Me ... dogboy ... dogboy ... al-ways."

Part of what he said was true, she could not deny it. Come what may, he would never be like other boys. The natural world—the world beyond the village—had stamped itself upon him. But to go through life as a dog ...! As a lowly animal and nothing else ...!

She tried objecting, tried explaining who he really was, but was drowned out by a series of barking cries. Not his. They came from a female dog crouched at his heels; the same animal he had grown up with.

He bent down and fondled her head.

"Sis-ster," he announced proudly. "Sis-ster ... to ... dogboy."

And Magda, meek by nature, could only bow her head in sad and grudging acceptance.

PART II

|the boy|

6

The news that the dogboy could speak changed the attitude of many of the villagers.

Phylo summed up the general feeling when he said: "Speech is the Great Father's gift to us. It is what stamps us as human; what separates us from the beasts. The fact that this boy can speak is therefore proof that he is in truth a boy."

"Then why was he reared by a dog?" Bartiss objected.

"That is a mystery which is still closed to us," Phylo admitted. "But I know this. Even though the child was reared as a beast, he has cast off his bestial ways. Through the act of speech he has declared himself human."

There was only one problem with Phylo's conclusion. The dogboy rejected it. Although his spoken language improved by the day, he continued to deny his human heritage. He denied it even in the face of his own instinctive need to speak; his own inner certainty about the order of words and the ancient rules that govern them.

"I am ... dog," he insisted stubbornly, and fingered the skull that he wore as a totem. "This my ... sign. I ... live for ... this only."

Magda was of the opinion that he was merely giving voice to his grief.

"He misses his dog-mother," she argued. "This is his way of expressing the loss he feels. Give him time, and he'll come round, you'll see. He'll begin to act like other boys his age."

For once, Nessa did not silence her servant. She openly agreed with her, which was something that had never happened before.

"Yes, patience is called for here," she added. "He'll need time to discover his true nature."

Old Sarah was even more generous. "If he's a boy, then we must give him a name. Once named, his human soul will become one with us. He will have no choice but to accept his humanity."

After a deal of discussion, the villagers decided on the name Jonas. But again they met with a problem: the dogboy refused to accept it.

"Dogs … no need … names," he told them. "Know by … smell … touch. Same for … dogboy."

Defeated, they left him to himself for a while, waiting for the winter cold. At the first hint of frost, they tried enticing him indoors, with offers of food and shelter, and good clothing to replace the skimpy loincloth he wore.

"It's cozy in here, out of the cold wind," they called. "There are fresh oatcakes waiting to be eaten."

His answer was to douse his own fire and huddle closer to his sister, in defiance of them. When they went on calling, he took once again to eating his meat raw. Even Magda's horrified protests had no effect on him. Tearing the flesh apart with his teeth, he would bolt down whole chunks in the manner of a dog.

The meat itself came from up on the mountain. Now that the mother dog was dead, he and his sister hunted for themselves. The moment they spied rabbits or rodents or other small animals, he would panic them by shouting and waving his arms—sometimes cutting off their retreat—

while she used her greater speed to run them down. Later, he added to their success by fashioning simple snares from wild rose stems and loops of twisted grass—inventions that he borrowed grudgingly from the villagers.

Together, he and his sister caught just enough for their needs. Meanwhile, there were also rose hips and berries for him to eat; and plums from the stunted trees that grew in the deeper gullies. He even found a tiny grove of almonds farther up the mountain, and gathered the nuts whenever they ventured near.

These frequent hunting trips were not without danger. Bears were a constant hazard. One, a battle-scarred male, charged them on a hot moon-drenched night, and it was only his sister, worrying bravely at the bear's heels, that allowed the dogboy to escape.

From a safe distance, he held his bear claw high and called through the moonlight: "See ... you, me ... we brothers."

A greater danger than bears were the wild dogs. More than once, they might have caught him but for his sister. With her finer sense of smell, she always sounded the alert in time for them to retreat to the village, though it was often a close-run thing. Panting, he would scramble up the wall just ahead of the pack, while his sister snapped and snarled at the lead dog.

"We ... same!" he would shout, showing them the skull he wore, and howl to the watchful stars.

One night his howling cries woke Magda, who went out to him.

"They'll kill you if you go on like this," she said.

He clambered down the wall and gazed at her sullenly. "Dog no ... kill ... this dog," he answered, stabbing at his chest.

"Then why do the village hounds stay inside the wall

when the packs are on the loose?" When he didn't reply, more sullen than ever, she went on: "You know why, don't you? Because they're scared of the packs. Because they're not wild like the others. They belong in here now. With us. With humans."

"Dogboy ... no belong," he insisted, clutching again at the skull he wore. "Not ... in village. Me ... belong ...," He flung one hand out vaguely, indicating the mysterious world of nature far beyond the wall.

"Who will take care of you out there?" she challenged him. "Who will keep you safe?"

He discovered an answer to that question some months later, when the peddler visited the village.

He had come that way once before, nine or ten years earlier, and he had looked younger then. Handsome, according to some, with a cheerful manner. Now, much older, gnarled by the weather and embittered by his poor, wandering life, he was a different kind of man. Outwardly, he still wore the same colorful clothing, his hat bedecked with bells; he still carried the same heavy pack, filled with cloth, needles and thread, printed ballads, and suchlike; but inside, he was wholly changed. A deep anger stirred within him, and as Magda recognized instantly, he had become a man to be reckoned with. Or better still, avoided.

Shucking off his pack in the village center, he surveyed the crowd that had gathered and noticed Magda among them. A knowing leer flitted across his face.

"It's been a long time," he said.

She detected the icy coolness beneath his smile.

"Not long enough," she said abruptly, and turned away.

"Ah, but long enough for you to lose your beauty," he called after her.

There were murmurs of disapproval from the crowd, and Phylo stepped forward.

"You're welcome here only so long as you keep a civil tongue in your head," he said sternly.

The peddler responded by tugging at his belled cap, in a mock show of humility. "You wouldn't cast out a lowly traveler, would you? A weary one at that. When all I'm looking for is a place to rest my bones awhile, and a chance to sell my wares. Fine wares they are too. The finest in the valley. I bought them myself in the great city of Delta."

The mention of Delta—a name only to most of them, and far distant from their village life—brought gasps of amazement from the younger villagers. The others seemed less impressed. Like Phylo, they continued to eye the peddler with distrust.

"Your wares are one thing," Phylo said. "Your cruel ways are another. We'll have none of those here."

"My word on it," the peddler vowed, and plucked off his hat in another show of humility. "The word of Joel the trader, the truest man this side of the great mountain."

"So you tell us," Phylo said doubtfully, but permitted him to unbuckle his pack and spread out its contents for all to see.

Looking on, the dogboy felt puzzled by Phylo's distrust. To his eyes, this Joel, as he called himself, was a wondrous figure. The boy had never heard anything like the tinkle of his belled cap; never seen anyone so flamboyantly dressed. And when Joel spread his wares, to reveal glittering rows of knives and scissors, colored ribbons in plenty, bright lengths of floral cloth, silver brooches and rings—the wonders went on and on—the dogboy was won over by the man entirely.

What was more, here was someone who lived outside

the village; who called the wider world his home. Why, he had even visited the fabled city of Delta, which the villagers spoke of in awed whispers; and which lay, some said, at the river's end.

The dogboy had only given his heart once before, to his dog mother; but now, dazzled by the man's cheap finery, he gave his heart to the peddler too. That night, he crept up to Joel's fire and placed a skinned rabbit at his feet, as a sign of homage.

"Why, what have we here?" Joel exclaimed, looking not at the rabbit, but at the near-naked boy. "A wild feller by the looks of you."

The dogboy nodded his agreement. "Yes ... wild ...," he repeated eagerly. "Like bear ... like eagle ... like ... like ..."

Joel interrupted him with a wink. "Not like these villagers, eh? Pretty tame lot they seem to me. Whereas *you* now ..." He spread both arms generously. "You strike me as a boy who's hoping for some excitement. Who doesn't want to live like other men. Who's looking for a little adventure, maybe, out there on the great road of life."

The dogboy had met no one as perceptive as this. How had the peddler guessed at his deepest wish? Or realized how different he was from the villagers?

"Here's an idea," Joel went on, and gave another wink. "What do you say to tagging along? As my helper. No, better still, as my apprentice. A strong lad like you is just what I need."

The dogboy did not understand words like *apprentice*, but he gathered that he was being given the chance to trot humbly at the peddler's heels; to act the part of the faithful dog he knew himself to be.

"Yes ... helper ...," he said happily. "Appre ... apprent ..." The word itself defeated him. But the idea of it! Overcome by emotion, he expressed his joy in the only other way he knew: by tipping back his head and baying like a hound.

Joel seemed delighted by the sound. Laughing to himself, he set about spitting the rabbit and hanging it above the coals.

"Yes, you'll do, my lad," he said with a chuckle. "You'll do very nicely for old Joel. You see if you don't."

7

They left the village at first light, only two days later. Joel strode out ahead, burdened with nothing heavier than a staff; the dogboy trudged at his heels, bent almost double under the weight of the pack; and his sister dog brought up the rear.

They had gone hardly any distance when Magda came running after them. She was barefoot, still in her nightshirt, her uncombed hair hanging around her shoulders. Breathless and angry, she had more the look of a mad woman than the meek servant the dogboy had always known.

"Shame on you!" she shouted at Joel, and barred the way. "He's a child, not a pack animal for you to make use of."

Joel tilted his cap so the bells rang merrily.

"Is that so?" he said in an offhand voice. "A child, you say. Well, that's news to me. And to him too. By his account, he's more animal than human, and he should know. What's more, I'm doing him a favor by rescuing him from the village. You don't believe me? Go on then, ask him yourself."

"You call this *rescuing* him?" she responded angrily. "Look at the boy, he's nearly broken in two by the weight. It's not right what you're doing, Joel."

The peddler's weathered features took on a hard look. "Don't tell me what's right," he said in a threatening voice. "Or you'll feel the back of my hand."

Magda maintained her defiance for a moment, and then

dropped her gaze. "I meant only that you walk the great world," she said in her usual, meek manner. "You understand the way of things more than the likes of us. You know how a child *should* be treated."

"Not … child!" the dogboy interrupted, having picked out that one word from all the talk. "Dogboy … me. Appren … apprent …"

Joel broke into harsh laughter. "You hear the boy? Because there you have it, Magda, from the babe's own lips. A peddler's apprentice, that's what he is."

Magda allowed herself a last flash of defiance. "He's no more an apprentice than I am! He's your dog, that's what. Your beast of burden. And don't tell me otherwise, because I know you, Joel. I know you well."

He moved forward aggressively, and tugged at Magda's graying hair, making her wince. "And I know you, Magda," he whispered. "Don't you forget it. Or I might be tempted to tell the boy here what you're really like."

She looked up at him, half defiant, half pleading. "No, leave the boy out of this. Let him find his own way."

He laughed again, less harshly, like a man without a care in the world. "His own way? But that's what I've been trying to tell you all along. He's chosen his path in life, and of his own free will. A path that begins here, in my wake. So out of our road, woman. He'll be a fine strapping man when you see him next. You can console yourself with that thought."

Magda showed no signs of being consoled. As they trudged away, she broke into tears and called after them: "Have a care of him, Joel. Please. He has no one now but you. If you don't look out for him, nobody will. Nobody, d'you hear?"

Her voice faded into the distance as they followed the river upstream, in the direction of the tallest mountain.

"There it is," Joel said grandly, pointing at the cloud-fringed peak. "The Great Father Himself."

The dogboy tried to look up but couldn't, the pack was too heavy. Not that he cared. He had never known a father, so what did they matter to him, great or small? Besides, in the peddler he had found more than a father—or so he believed. He had discovered a hero: someone who would lead him through life, much as he led his sister hound. The important thing—the only thing that mattered for the present—was to please this hero. And so he walked bravely on, his legs quaking under the fearful weight of the pack.

But for all his determination, he was still less than ten years old; strong for his years, but a child just the same. Try as he might, he couldn't match the peddler's loping pace. After two hours ... three ... he began to stagger and fall behind.

Joel, never a patient man, let a little of his true character show. "Keep up, damn you!" he roared. And an hour later, when the weary boy slowed more, he cut a switch from a clump of reeds in the shallows and flogged him across the legs. "Get on with you now," he said in a steely voice.

The dogboy did not resent being flogged. He had seen dogs beaten in the village. It was clearly their fate. So why should he be treated any differently? He was failing in his task, after all, and deserved this punishment.

Somehow, despite his fatigue, he managed to keep going. Through a fog of weariness, he staggered as far as a settlement in a neighboring valley, which they reached in midafternoon.

There, he found little rest. While the peddler showed off his wares, he was left to set up camp and prepare their evening meal. Again he obeyed, driving himself on. At sunset, he dutifully handed the peddler his food, and was tossed a few scraps in return. They landed in the dust at his feet, but by then he was almost too tired to eat. Sinking down, he reached for the first of the scraps ... and was asleep before he could raise it to his mouth.

Unseen by him, his sister hound bolted down the rest.

"Get off, you cur!" the peddler snarled, aiming a kick at her ribs.

The dogboy heard nothing of this. Caught up in a distant dream, he was running on all fours across the wind-swept mountain, following the resplendent figure of Joel, who bounded ahead.

"Keep up!" Joel shouted joyously, and pointed to a golden dip in the hills that seemed to beckon them on.

They never reached the golden place. The cool, far harsher light of day broke through the dream, and the dogboy woke to a well-delivered blow on the ear.

With his head ringing, he stumbled up and began preparing a simple breakfast of oatcakes. When the oatcakes were done, the peddler snatched up most of them, and left just two.

"They're for you alone. Understand?" he said gruffly. "Not for that moth-eaten cur who limps after us."

The boy looked at his sister dog, and back at the peddler. "She ... she hungry ... same us," he said, convinced that he'd be listened to.

Joel's response was to hit him across the ear a second time. It was a harder blow than before, and the boy almost snarled and snapped at the offending hand. What restrained him was his lingering admiration for the peddler. How could such a man be cruel, he asked himself? Or greedy? No, Joel was probably testing him; discovering the limits of his obedience.

Even so, he could not resist slipping a cake to his sister,

and keeping only one for himself. With that meager meal to sustain him, he again shouldered the pack and followed the peddler from the settlement.

Their present route proved more grueling than the previous day's. Joel had it in mind to visit a far-flung valley. To reach it, they had to climb up over the northern shoulder of the great mountain and down through what he called the "Sad Lands," the most barren area in the whole region.

Time and again, as they labored up the steepening slopes, the dogboy faltered.

"Get on!" Joel shouted, slashing at his legs with the switch. "What good are you if you can't bear the weight of the pack? I might as well carry it myself and leave you here to rot."

The threat of being abandoned or found wanting kept the dogboy going for most of the day. His actual strength was soon exhausted, but his will, stronger by far than his unformed body, refused to break. Half-blind with weariness, he tottered from ridge to ridge in the mounting heat of the afternoon.

He was not aware of topping the highest point and taking a downward path. Each pace was an agony by then. Up or down, backwards or sideways, meant nothing to him. The breeze alone he was grateful for. It sprang up toward evening, deliciously cool on his sweat-stained body, like a message of sympathy from the Great Father Himself.

"Thank … you," he murmured through cracked lips, and slumped to his knees in the shadow-streaked dust.

Joel tried beating him, as he'd done all day, but it did no good. The boy's sister snarled and growled a warning in the background, and the peddler cursed her in reply. As for the dogboy, he lay fast asleep where he had fallen, the pack still strapped to his shoulders.

He awoke, many hours later, to aching limbs and a dawn as gray and forbidding as the surrounding hills. He sat up in the dust and stared out over the "Sad Lands." Was this the outer world he had yearned for? This place of bone-dry gullies and bone-hard crags, where nothing grew, not even a few twigs of withered thyme or wild rose?

He switched his gaze to the peddler, who lay stretched on the ground nearby. His face, in the same gray dawn light, was not unlike the land itself: seamed and weathered by the years; all the beauty, all the gentleness, eroded away. And sad also, marked by the misery of lost hope and defeat.

In those first few minutes of consciousness, the dogboy lost his awe of this man he had claimed as a hero. Moved by a sudden rush of pity, he came close to feeling sorry for him. But then the peddler woke and fixed him with his unloving gaze.

"What are you gawping at?" he grumbled. "There's a fire to be lit. Or have you gone completely idle on me?"

The boy indicated the bare hillsides. "No wood … no fire."

"What?" The peddler's cheeks bloomed an angry pink. "Is the brat answering me back now?"

"No wood … no fire," the dogboy repeated stoutly.

"Then go out there and find some wood, damn you!" came the reply, and the peddler reached for his switch.

Still the dogboy did not resist. Hunched down under the blows, he was determined to endure. But not his sister. As the peddler dropped the switch and began using his fists, she sprang to the attack.

"You want some too, do you!" Joel yelled, and began kicking her instead.

Normally, she would have sprung away, but they were camped in the blind end of a gully, the rocky face rising steeply on three sides. Trapped, all she could do was yelp and snarl and try to dodge the blows. Many found their mark, and one sent her reeling, too dazed to rise.

That was when the dogboy acted. He had not been ready to defend himself—not yet—but his sister …! His friend and only kin …! Touching his hand to the skull he wore, he sprang onto the peddler's back; sank his teeth into the gnarled skin of his neck; raked at his eyes.

He was flung aside within seconds, no match for a grown man. Like his sister, he was trapped within the gully and soundly beaten.

Bleeding and bruised, they were left twined together on the rocky ground, while Joel hoisted the pack to his shoulders.

"A lot of good you turned out to be!" he said. "Well, here's farewell to you both." And with those words—the last they ever heard from his mouth—he trudged off.

Boy and dog took time to lick their wounds and gather their wits. They had no food, no water, and little strength after their recent ordeal. Yet far harder to bear than all of this was the dogboy's painful sense of disappointment. His hero had turned out to be no hero at all, but a sad and bitter man. Why, he was no better than people like Bartiss or Nessa. Worse perhaps, because at least they didn't pretend to be kindly or caring. They were what they were; whereas the peddler, with his colorful clothing and cheerful manner, was a sly trickster. And to think that he, the dogboy, had been ready to trot humbly at his heels! To be beaten and ruled by him! To call him master!

The boy was still not fluent enough to put these thoughts into words. He came to a decision just the same. Never again would he play the part of the faithful hound; never would he call another human being master. If he had to live the life of a dog, he would be proud and defiant. More like the wild dogs high on the mountain. Not cruel like them, or savage, but untamed.

"Come," he said with a groan, and rose stiffly to his feet.

His sister, more badly injured than he, could only whimper in reply. No matter, he thought. Lifting her up, he draped her gently across his shoulders. She weighed less than the pack and was far more precious, so he didn't complain. This, he decided, was the price he must pay for his foolishness.

With the sun warm on his battered limbs, he turned toward the great mountain, determined to retrace his steps.

8

They limped back into the village a week later. Where else was there for them to turn? Still bruised and sore, walking side by side, they greeted no one, not even Magda, who gave a shriek of joy at their return.

Let the villagers think and say what they pleased—he had decided this too. He, the dogboy, would ignore them; he would use this place as a shelter and nothing else. In his heart, if not in fact, he would be as free and untroubled by men as the packs of wild dogs. They had always fascinated him, since earliest childhood, and now he would take them as his guiding star. He, too, would remain fiercely independent of all human touch.

Deaf to the occasional cry of welcome, he stalked through the village and set up camp beside his old firestones, over near the outer wall. He was building a crude shelter for himself and his sister when Magda went to him later in the day.

She took quiet note of his scabbed face and back. "I see he beat you," she said sadly.

He gave her an angry look, and she guessed then that he was not the same boy who had set out so hopefully with Joel.

"Yes ... beat," he agreed. "One day ... one day ... I beat ... I!"

"Then you'll be as bad as he is. Is that what you want?"

"He man," he answered her. "I dog. Two … not same bad."

"But a dog who can speak. Who can think. Who can control fire. These things will make you a man one day, say what you please."

He rounded on her, angrier than ever, his eyes dark with passion. "I … please … no one! Not … him … not … you … no one! I … master now … I pack leader."

"Yes, I can see you are," she said wearily, and sat by his freshly laid fire.

He waved her away, but she took no notice, sitting there silently until he had calmed down.

"Long ago," she explained, "he disappointed me too. So I know how you feel."

But he wouldn't accept that either. "I … feel like … like dog. You … like human. Different."

"We're all different," she admitted. "Even Joel. Because he wasn't always this way. Cruel and uncaring. Once he was young, handsome. Not selfish and horrible, like now. You should try to remember that. It will help you hate him less."

"I … hate!" he insisted. "Hate … all people."

She shook her head and sighed. "I don't believe you. I won't."

In the months that followed his return, however, he tested her faith in him. Cold, aloof, he acted as if the other villagers did not exist. When people offered food or fuel for his fire, he turned his back. Kind words he sneered at; angry ones made him laugh scornfully.

Magda he treated with special disdain. "You … slave," he told her. "Same … for me … before. Me … learn. You … no learn. You … tame dog. No … bite."

"And you?" she answered tearfully. "Do you bite?"

He said nothing to that, just bared his teeth in a cold smile.

His attitude to other animals was different entirely. His sister he treated with unfailing kindness, sharing everything with her. Together they roamed the lower slopes—hunting at night, frolicking and mock-fighting in the cool of the morning. They still fled from the wild packs, and with good reason, but once safely in the village, he would stand on the wall and howl to his wild cousins for hours at a time.

The villagers soon began to lose patience.

"Give him back to the river, that's what I say," Nessa announced one day. "Wait for the next flood, and throw him in. Let's see how scornful he is then, when the current takes him."

"Better still," Bartiss added, "if he likes those wild dogs so much, why not give him to *them*? They'd make short work of him, and we'd be done with his scorn once and for all."

There were plenty of such suggestions at around that time, though most were not meant seriously. Not to begin with. But as each fresh moon waxed and waned, the mood in the village grew more ugly.

Had things continued in this way, he might well have been cast out. Or he might have left of his own free will: walked off into the mountains with his sister and rejected humanity forever. Before any of that could happen, something intervened—a rescue of sorts.

He had been saved once before, by the river in flood. Now, he was saved from becoming an outcast by a very different force: one more savage than the river could ever be. And the rescue itself—if you can call it that—nearly cost him his life.

He and his sister were hunting in the hills one evening

when a wild pack got wind of them. They heard the lead hounds baying farther up the gully, and should instantly have run off. But the dogboy was perched in one of his beloved almond trees, gathering nuts, and he stole a few precious moments in order to fill the side pocket of the satchel.

When he eventually climbed down, he guessed straight-away that he had delayed too long. The hounds sounded much nearer now, and his sister was visibly nervous, dancing away down the slope. He followed her as fast as he dared, pacing himself so as not to tire too soon. The pack, he knew, could easily outrun him over a long distance. His one chance was to start out with a good lead—except that in this instance much of his lead had already been squandered back there among the trees.

Less than halfway down the mountain, he glanced over his shoulder and glimpsed the main body of the pack. They were not far behind, their coats shimmering in the moonlight. And the rest? The outriders? He looked to his right and saw them: the fiercest and the fastest of the dogs, angling across the hillside to cut him off. There were more dogs to his left, also angling in. He had no option but to increase his pace, though he knew he might pay dearly for that in the end.

He was right. Well short of the village, he was forced to slow, his breath whistling in his lungs. It was then that the pack closed in. There was a yelp as his sister was bowled over by the pack leader, and seconds later they were upon him.

He felt pain in his thigh, and he went down. He tried to rise, but was slashed across the throat, and fell again. Dimly, he was aware of his sister huddling close, her body trembling against his; while all around the pack gathered for the kill.

Had he tried to fight them off, or even curled up into a

ball, he would have died. The first few dogs came lunging in, slashing at him, and he did what his dog mother had taught him years earlier. He flipped onto his back, arms held wide, and bared his throat to his attackers. It was the accepted sign of submission—one that nearly all dogs respect. Beside him, his sister had done the same, both of them defenseless.

Still the pack lunged in, but always they balked at the last moment, their instincts telling them to hold off. Last of all, the lead dog came and stood above him, his ruff bristling, his fangs exposed. Remembering his early training, the dogboy did not meet the leader's eye—aware that eye contact alone could have signaled an attack.

For long seconds, neither of them moved: the lead dog rumbling deep in his throat; the dogboy careful to show no resistance. Then, as abruptly as they had arrived, the pack was gone, racing back toward the mountain.

He waited until their baying voices had faded into the distance before trying to rise. One leg, he found, would not hold his weight, the whole thigh laid open. There were similar wounds on various parts of his body, but the wound in his throat was the worst: a great gash that stretched from one ear down to his breastbone. His sister was in a similar state, each of them leaving behind a thin trail of blood as they struggled on toward the village.

It was the loss of blood that most threatened them. With every passing minute they grew weaker. So weak that when they reached the wall, they had barely strength enough to clamber up and topple into the safety of the village.

The dogboy had not sought help from anyone since the days of the peddler. He had been too proud. Too determined to stand alone. Even now, it was only his sister's plight that broke down his pride. Unable to help her himself, he did the only other thing he could: he appealed to Magda.

She heard his faint voice calling to her through the night, and when she went out, she found him and his so-called sister lying nearly dead by the wall. Both had been badly mauled and were unable to rise, so she dragged them one by one into the makeshift shelter the dogboy himself had built. There, she cared for them in the days that followed: watching as they both slipped into unconsciousness; waiting uncertainly for their fevers to break.

The bitch was the first to recover. Stiff from her wounds, which Magda had stitched closed, she tottered from the shelter and lay sprawled in the warm sun.

The dogboy remained unconscious much longer, gripped by a fever that refused to break. Time and again, Magda lanced his festering wounds, convinced that they were poisoning his entire system, and each time the infection returned. Finally, she undid all her careful stitching and laid bare his torn flesh; then packed the open wounds with crushed herbs and closed them again.

Two nights later, the fire in his body died down and his eyes flicked open. Feebly, through bloodless lips, he called for water. Weeping tears of relief, Magda held the cup to his mouth; smoothed the sweat-stiffened hair from his face with loving hands.

"Welcome ...," she whispered tearfully. "Welcome ..."

Weak though he was, he looked up at her with puzzled eyes. Why should she weep for him? Why should any human care whether he lived or died? Her attitude was a mystery, but for all that he felt glad. Happy to be free of the dark world of delirium that had held him for days; happier still to feel her hands warm upon his face and to know he was no longer alone.

It took him weeks to recover fully, and during most of that time he was dependent on Magda. He resented this at first. But slowly he came to accept that he needed her, much as his sister needed him, and with acceptance came a softening of his proud spirit. Not all humans were like the peddler; nor all dogs like the wild packs on the mountain. There were also people like Magda, animals like his sister, who could be relied on, looked to for help and support. No, more than that: there were creatures other than himself that he could not live without.

Humbled by his experience, he took to smiling at the passing villagers as he sat in the healing sunlight. He would spend hours at a time talking to the local children—whom he had utterly ignored until then. They in turn helped him speak more clearly. And when they couldn't answer all his questions, no less a man than Phylo came to sit with him.

Phylo had also softened in recent years. He remembered with a degree of shame how he had once rejected the dogboy, and seemed eager to make amends.

"So what can I tell you today?" he would ask, squatting in the dust at the boy's side.

Mostly, he explained the history of the village and how it depended on the mercy of the Great Father who brought rain and made the river flow. And how their unquestioning faith in the Spirit of the Great Mountain was the keystone of their lives, sustaining them through any hardship. At other times he sketched out what little he knew of Delta, the fabled city that stood at river's end—describing its great mansions and rustling palm trees, and many of its other wonders. But for all his willingness to teach the boy, there were two questions he could not answer, the most pressing questions of all as far as the dogboy was concerned.

"My parents … tell me who … which people …?" he asked repeatedly, and always saw the same baffled expression creep across Phylo's face.

"You were given to us by the Great Father," Phylo answered carefully. "He sent you here on the river. As to why you came, and from where, or for what purpose, these things are beyond my reckoning."

"So tell ... tell me other thing," the dogboy pressed him. "What ... am I? Boy or dog? I look same boy ... This I know. But ... *inside*? What like in there?"

"Why, a boy, what else?"

"Then why ... dog mother? Why ... dog sister?" He sniffed the air; made a soft growling sound. "Why I *feel* ... same dog?"

The baffled look returned to Phylo's face. "Who can say?" he muttered uneasily. "These are mysteries that only the Great Father can solve. When the storm clouds gather on the mountain, listen for His voice in the thunder."

The dogboy had already tried listening to the thunder, and heard no voice at all: only the grinding together of earth and sky.

In desperation, he put the same two puzzling questions to Magda. Surprisingly, she dismissed them both.

"Who your parents are doesn't matter. The important thing is that you're special."

"Special ... how?"

"The Great Father, He sent you here for a purpose. For a reason."

"What this ... this *reason*?"

"Aah." She looked at him archly. "That's something you have yet to find out. All you have to do is wait. Be patient, and life will give you the answer."

Patience was a lot to ask of a half-grown boy. On the one hand, he yearned to choose a road. Yet when he looked ahead, two roads seemed to fork away into the mist. Along one, he walked as a boy; along the other, he trotted as a dog.

Which to take?

As baffled as Phylo, he found himself living in two worlds at once. By day, he lived quietly among the other villagers; by night, in the company of his sister, he took to scouring the mountain once again, armed with a homemade sling and spear. Except he knew now that he didn't belong there any longer, not as the wild dogs belonged. Nor did he belong wholly in the village. Torn between the two, he felt lost. Confused. Someone with two separate selves, each pitted against the other.

Late at night, on the verge of sleep, he asked himself over and over: "Which way ...? Which ...?"

His only answer was the rumble of thunder from the far-off peaks.

9

Young as he was, he stood at the pivotal point of his life. Rather than blunder forward blindly, he turned instead to those he cared for. To Magda, who had nursed him back to health. To the only parent he knew, the Great Father, whom he addressed in silent prayer. And to his sister, his one sure link to the mysterious past.

She was over ten now, old for a dog, and had never had any young. Then all at once, and as though adding to the mystery of his life, she fell pregnant.

"It can't be," Magda said doubtfully. "She's too old. More than seventy by our way of counting."

Yet her belly continued to expand; her teats to swell. And one hot morning, she padded down to the dry riverbed and dug for herself a cool den in the shadow of a rocky outcrop. There, at nightfall, she gave birth to three pups: two males, who mewed once and died; and a female, puny but alive.

"Quick," Magda advised, when she and the dogboy found the live puppy there the next morning, her dead brothers beside her. "Give her a name. It will hold her here in the world of the living."

He bit his lip, unsure.

"I not ... have name," he argued. "Why ... this one?"

"Look at her," Magda said. "She's weak, not strong like you. You don't need a name, but she does."

Still he hesitated. This tiny creature was his kin—the

granddaughter of the dog he had called mother. It felt wrong to give her a name when he possessed none himself. As he saw it, naming things was a human act: a way of binding them to the human world. To name this pup would therefore tie her to the village forever; deny her the wild birthright which was rightly hers.

Magda, standing silently beside him, seemed to understand his dilemma.

"Are you scared a name will tame her?" she asked.

He nodded.

"Then give her a daytime name. A village name. One she leaves behind when she goes off into the hills at night."

What Magda said seeped down into his innermost thoughts. For at eleven years old, he also had a secret hankering for a name, despite all his denials. Not Jonas, once bestowed on him by the villagers—that was too close to the hated name of Joel. What he needed was some other word, a simple sound, that would serve as a link between him and people, and yet not bind him to them.

"Well …?" Magda said.

He gave her the most truthful answer he could.

"I … Boy," he said, pressing a hand to his chest. "She … she Girl."

Magda smiled and kissed him fleetingly on the cheek.

"Yes, that's good. Boy … I like it. Girl, too. And look." She pointed down into the den. "The pup, she understands what you've done."

For already Girl was struggling toward the teat, which she latched onto and began to suck at greedily.

She went from strength to strength after that. Though with each passing day the mother grew weaker. On the morning that Girl first ventured onto the riverbed alone, her mother died quietly in her sleep.

"It was her time," Magda explained sadly. "She was too old to give birth. It wore her out; it sapped what strength she had left. She's better off now. She deserves this rest."

Boy was inconsolable. "She … sister," he said brokenly. "Only … one."

Ignoring the helpless pup that whined for attention, he picked up the dead body and carried it to his shelter near the outer wall. There, dry-eyed with misery, he sat and cradled it in his arms, exactly as he had once cradled his dog mother.

For three days he sat, unmoving, never giving way to grief. Though once, in the stillness of the night, he felt sadness, like a dark tide, rising up through his body. He looked to the stars, and saw them through a blur of tears, while over in the mountains, lightning flickered, thunder rolled, and storm clouds gathered. But then he blinked away his tears, stony-faced once more—unaware of how the thunder faded back into the silence.

By evening of the third day, the smell from the decaying body began wafting through the village.

Bartiss was all for pitching them both over the wall, Boy and carcass together.

"No, give him time," Magda pleaded.

"Time?" Bartiss complained. "Hasn't he had plenty of that already? This is a dog he's mourning, a dead animal, not a real sister. One more hot day, and he'll bring the plague down upon us."

There *had* been a plague in the village once, many years earlier, and it had carried off nearly half the children. Those old enough to remember it sided with Bartiss.

"Yes," they shouted. "It's our children who'll be paying for his grief next."

Although Phylo had also experienced the plague, he chose to act as peacemaker.

"You're right," he said. "We can't endure another day of that smell. Not now, at the height of summer. It would be dangerous. But one more night will do no harm. Give the boy until dawn. It's only right to let him walk the road of grief to its very end."

As it happened, Boy did not need until dawn. Close to midnight, he hefted the dead body over the wall and laid it out on the stone cairn he had built for his mother. The rest of the night he spent howling at the stars.

Soon after first light the vultures arrived. Magda heard them squabbling over the carcass as the day advanced. She thought she knew what would happen next: how one morning Boy would appear with a second skull hanging from his necklace.

Yet he had always been able to surprise her, and he did so now. When he approached her hut, he wore only the original skull and the other charms he had gathered in early childhood. In his fist, however, he held a short length of string with a single eyetooth threaded on it.

"Where … Girl?" he demanded.

Magda had rescued the pup from the riverbed and weaned her since then. Flipping aside some old rags, she revealed her sleeping body in the shadow of the hut. She looked much sturdier now: a stocky little animal who opened one eye and gazed lazily up at them.

Boy took her in his hands and tied the string with the eyetooth around her neck. She fought against it at first, clawing the string with her front paws until he bent forward and mouthed the word "mother." That word seemed to calm her—or perhaps it was just his tone of voice—because moments later she curled up in the crook of his arm and went back to sleep.

They were inseparable after that. If Magda called to

one, both arrived on her doorstep. Nessa, as usual, disapproved of their bonding and called it unnatural, but Phylo laughed and said they were rightly named.

"The whole world is made up of male and female things," he declared wisely. "Together they make a whole. So it is with these two."

Whether Phylo was right or not was of little interest to Boy, who reveled in his new pup. At six months, she began following him up the mountain, and at a year she was big and strong enough to hunt down rabbits. The wild packs still posed a threat, but Boy never again made the mistake of running from them. When he heard their baying in the hills nearby, he looked for a blind gully to protect his back; then spear or sling in hand, with Girl at his side, he prepared to fight them off.

They only once attacked in earnest. The lead hound charged in, and found his shoulder spitted on the fire-hardened tip of Boy's spear. The rest were driven off by a few well-aimed flints from the sling, while Girl, her hackles up, harried the heels of any stragglers.

Like her grandmother, Girl matured into a dog to be reckoned with. She would back down to nothing on the mountain, not even the great bears who occasionally ambled from the heights in search of rose hips and berries. Whenever they encountered one, Boy had to call her off.

"Hush," he would whisper, and let her sniff the claw or the bear tooth he wore. "He … friend … to Boy … to Girl … to Great Father. We … no fight."

Like Boy, she soon learned the ways of the mountain. Back in the village, they were less sure of themselves. Boy, for instance, still spoke falteringly, as though wrestling with a foreign tongue.

"It's time you spoke like other boys," Magda told him.

"You're quick enough to learn everything else."

"Me … not same … other boys," he said proudly.

"I know, you're special," she said with a smile. "But you could still try and speak like them."

"Not same," he insisted.

She took him by the chin and gently forced him to meet her eyes. "What are you telling me? That you don't *want* to learn?"

He refused to answer, still proudly defiant in this one thing.

"All right, go and be special in your own way then," she said with a laugh, and left him to speak as he pleased.

Privately—although he refused to show it—he felt bothered by that word "special." What did it mean? How would it reveal itself? Or was it something that Magda had just imagined? Here was a mystery as deep as the mystery of his true origins, and he worried about it constantly.

The villagers, on the other hand, had more pressing matters to concern them. In particular, the drought, which had closed its fist upon the land once more. A full year passed without rain; then another. What was left of the river sank away into the sand; the crops shriveled and died; at night, the wail of hungry children could again be heard from the huts.

Boy helped as best he could. He brought extra meat from the mountain and shared it among the most needy families. He helped dig wells deeper and deeper into the riverbed. He even offered to show Phylo where water could be found more easily, farther downstream. Except Phylo could not be bothered to listen: he thought he knew the ways of the river better than any dogboy—an overgrown child who could not even learn to speak their tongue.

"Yes … yes," he said vaguely, and wandered away.

"Me … special!" Boy called after him. "Me … show."

"Yes … later," Phylo called back, closing his ears to Boy's claims.

Nobody else would listen either. For them, the finding of water was a serious business, not to be entrusted to a weird dogboy who had appeared from heaven knows where. They had other plans for the future. They had heard from a passing messenger of a powerful shaman who was visiting settlements along the valley. A rainmaker no less, who owned a great house in the city of Delta.

"He's the one to ease our suffering," Phylo decided. "No shaman acquires wealth unless he has the ear of the Great Father."

"He *and* his wife," Nessa put in with a nod. "From what I hear, she has the powers of a witch, and adds her spells to his."

But when would they arrive—that was the question—and would they be in time to save the village? Clearly, someone had to go and search them out; to lure them back with what little gold the villagers possessed.

Boy offered to go, but was rejected.

"Be quiet now," old Sarah told him. "This is grown-up talk."

Bartiss pushed him roughly aside. "Yes, we're deciding on a task for a man, not a dogboy."

It was finally agreed that Bartiss himself would go. He set out early the next morning, waved off by the whole village. Boy was the only one absent from the cheering throng.

To him, it seemed absurd, asking strangers for help. Even rich strangers from Delta—if such a place really existed. How could they or anyone make the Great Father listen? How could they possibly bring rain? Rain was a gift freely bestowed—*he* knew that—a gift from the Father of all mountains to the land below. Hadn't he seen storm clouds roll in from the heights? Hadn't he heard thunder instructing them to release their watery load? That was something no shaman could do, whatever his skills.

Filled with disbelief, Boy spat into the dust and waited, listening hard. The breeze blew, rattling the dry thatch of the huts; a few surviving hens scratched busily in the dirt; a village dog nipped at his belly, hunting for fleas. These were familiar sounds, all of them. And beyond those sounds … silence. No word from the distant mountain.

Boy smiled quietly to himself. Yes, it was just as he suspected. The Great Father slept. *That* was the true meaning of this prolonged drought, and no man, shaman or otherwise, could wake Him before His time.

10

Bartiss returned the day after the dust storm. People were still shaking sandy grit from their clothes and bedding when he led the two strangers into the village.

The man was called Arron, his wife Elvina, and they were both tall and magnificently dressed in scarlet robes that reached almost to their ankles. Around Arron's neck hung a necklace of clear crystals that had been shaped into the likeness of raindrops. Elvina wore a similar string of stones, though hers were smaller and looped across her forehead. Each had a single tattoo on the right cheek, of the river god—shaped like a coiled snake, its two red eyes glowing.

They greeted the villagers with a simple message of hope: "We bring promise of rain."

"May the Great Father bless you for this," Phylo sobbed gratefully.

"To see this valley green again," Elvina said grandly, "that will be blessing enough for us."

With the people looking on, she called for dry clay and water. From these, she and her husband began fashioning a crude likeness of the village itself, a task which occupied most of the afternoon.

While they worked, the villagers came and went, busy with their own daily tasks. Boy was the only one among them who did not wander off. Squatting in the dust, as close to the two visitors as he dared, he watched their every move with wondering eyes.

He had been enthralled by a colorfully dressed stranger once before, and had vowed never to be taken in again. But not in all his wild imaginings had he pictured to himself people like this. Why, compared to them, Joel the peddler had looked cheap and tawdry, in his crudely dyed cotton clothes and his cap with its half-rusted bells. Here were people altogether different, with robes of shimmering silk and glittering necklaces. Not tricksters, but true rainmakers: magical figures, skilled in the great mysteries that baffled even someone as old as Phylo.

Coming and going with the rest, Magda noticed the awed look on Boy's face and felt her heart contract.

"Remember what happened with Joel," she warned him in a whisper. "Don't make the same mistake again. Let them be, now."

He shook her off impatiently. How could she liken the peddler to this wondrous couple? Did she have no eyes? No faith or trust? No belief in what was good?

"Not ... same ... Joel," he hissed back at her. "Same ... same ..."—he paused, hunting for a true comparison—"same ... like mountain."

He spoke with such conviction that there was no point in arguing, and she left him to his vigil.

He was still squatting there at sunset when the villagers set up flares all around and gathered to watch. There was just light enough in the western sky to reveal the storm clouds hovering above the highest peaks; and without needing to be told, the people knew that the shaman and his wife would try to lure those clouds closer to the foothills where the river had its source.

The ritual was begun by Arron, who drew the shape

of a triangle around the finished model. At each point of the triangle, he placed a sacred object: a tiny stone carving of the Earth Mother; a sphere of clear glass, with a piece of thistledown trapped inside; and a splinter of black opal, which caught and held the light from the flares. Together, they represented the three eternal forces: earth, air, and fire. Only the fourth force was missing—water—and this was supplied by Elvina.

She did not add another sacred object to the triangle. Instead, she started to dance. It was a well-known dance of loss, of a mother grieving for a dead child, and she performed it with a passion that brought tears to the villagers' eyes. She also wept toward the end, allowing her tears to sprinkle over the clay model of the village.

The dance over, every eye turned toward the storm clouds. Were they any nearer? It was hard to tell, the dusk thickening, the distant peaks all but hidden by the dark. Yet the people returned to their huts with high hopes, Boy among them.

That night, he did not hunt on the mountain. Lying in his shelter, Girl curled up at his side, he prayed silently for the Great Father to be moved by Elvina's dance and for His tears to fall as rain. Already, it did not occur to Boy that the drought might continue. Or that the rain, when it came, could fall anywhere but on the village. For hadn't Arron hedged the village in with the three eternal forces? Hadn't he guaranteed that it would rain here and nowhere else?

Despite his faith, the next day dawned perfectly clear. As clear as nearly every morning over the past few years.

"No matter," Arron told the assembled villagers. "We will try again. Day by day, we will bind the forces of earth and sky to our will."

So for the next three evenings the ritual was repeated, always with the same negative result. By the fourth day, people began muttering among themselves. That afternoon, when the villagers gathered at the riverbed wells to collect water, there were open expressions of discontent.

"These Delta folk are all the same," Nessa grumbled. "Full of grand promises, and that's about all."

"Aye," old Sarah said gloomily. "But they'll expect payment in gold whatever the outcome."

For once, Bartiss didn't join in the general complaint. Partly because he was the one who had searched out these rainmakers. Partly, too, because in his youth he had failed as a shaman and understood the bitterness of defeat.

"Let them have a last try," he pleaded. "We have much at stake here, for if it doesn't rain soon, we'll all end up as beggars ... or worse."

That evening, the ritual took place as usual, though it seemed to Boy that Elvina performed her dance of loss with particular passion, her tears falling on the clay model like the rain they all yearned for.

Surely the Great Father will listen to them now, he thought, as he lay awake in his shelter. He hated the idea of their failing. In his orphaned state, he saw in these two people an image of the parents he had always dreamed of. Were they to suffer defeat ... to slink from the village in shame ...? No! He could not let that happen! Could not bear even to consider it. Except who was he—a lowly dogboy—to influence the lives of the mighty? Least of all to rescue them from shame?

In his anguished state, he crawled from the shelter and gazed up at the night sky. Mostly it was clear, but over toward the mountain stood a dense band of black. And yes, he could just make out faint flickers of lightning, followed long after by distant rumblings. So there *was* still hope of rain, if only … if only …

In a desperate attempt to help these longed-for parent figures, he slipped the stone from the string around his neck and peered at it in the pale starlight. It was the same stone which he, as a baby, had plucked from the depths of the wild river. Magda had told him often enough that it contained a potent force. The power of the flooding river, no less.

But did it?

Now, it seemed, was the time to find out. Silently, he padded through the village until he came to the clay model. There it sat, guarded by its magic triangle and its three sacred objects. Compared with those sacred things, his own small stone appeared a poor offering. Yet it was all he had, and he gave it freely. First he spat on it for luck, and then placed it at the very center of the model.

That done, he returned to his shelter and slept through the rest of the night.

He awoke to a patter of rain on the thatch overhead. It was nearly dawn, and quickly, before anyone else woke, he ran across to the model and rescued his stone. In the gray light of early morning, his belief in its power seemed foolish—vain even—and he felt glad that no one had seen him put it there.

It was raining in earnest as he slipped it back on the string around his neck. The roar of the storm, and its accompanying thunder, brought people hurrying from their huts. Overjoyed at the cloudburst, they laughed and sang and danced on the now muddy earth.

"The Great Father be praised," Phylo sang out. "It's time for planting again."

With the rain still teeming down, he called to Arron and Elvina, who emerged in all their finery.

"Our task here is complete," Arron announced with a

smile. "There are others farther down the valley who await our help."

"And fortunate they are too," Bartiss said loudly—more delighted by the rainmakers' success than anyone.

"Aye, they'd be fools not to place their faith in you," old Sarah cried, forgetting her earlier doubts.

There and then, Phylo produced the agreed payment in gold and offered it humbly. Elvina whisked it from his hand and secreted it somewhere beneath her robe.

"Your generosity is great," she said shortly, mouthing the time-honored words. "We are in debt to you."

Phylo answered her in the accepted fashion, though with more grace: "It is we who are in debt, and ever shall be."

She flashed him a brief smile, and turned away as Arron reached for her hand, their faces set toward home.

Boy, in the forefront of the crowd, had realized that this moment must come, but had not expected it so soon. He felt a knot of panic tighten inside him. He had only just found these wonderful people, and already he was about to lose them! How would he endure life in the village once they had gone? How could he let them slip away like this?

Summoning his courage, he ran and tugged at Elvina's robe.

She spun around, her face hard at first, but then softened by the same brief smile she had offered Phylo. "Yes, boy?"

The audacity of what he was about to do almost stopped his breath. "You ... you go ... Delta?"

"Of course. Where else? It's where we live."

He pressed fingertips to his bare chest. "I ... go too?"

"If you wish. Delta is an open city. Anyone can go there."

He shook his head. "No ... I go ... with you."

It was Arron who answered him. "We aren't making

straight for the city. We have several other stops to make. You'd do better to complete the journey alone."

"Come away, Boy," Nessa called from behind, her voice faint through the rain. "Give the shaman some peace. He deserves it after all he's done for us."

"There, the good woman's calling you," Arron said, not unkindly. "Go to her."

Yet having ventured this far, Boy could not simply give up. Clutching hard onto Elvina's robe, he made one last appeal.

"I … I go … Delta … I see … you in … your house? You help … Boy?"

Elvina flicked her skirt from his hand, while Arron bowed low, an extravagant gesture that brought laughter from the watching villagers.

"It is our dearest wish to turn none from our door," he said evenly. "But there are many who are poor and needy in Delta. Many, you understand?"

Then they were gone, as though swallowed by the rain, leaving behind only their footprints in the mud.

Boy walked dejectedly back to the waiting villagers. Gathered in the downpour, hair plastered to their skulls, their clothes sodden, they appeared a sorry bunch compared with Arron and Elvina. Looking at them, Boy felt more than ever that he had allowed his true life—the one he yearned for—to seep like water between his fingers.

As he passed through the crowd, Nessa jeered: "What would such fine folk want with a dogboy?"

And Bartiss: "You should have told them about your mother. *That* would have impressed them."

Others mocked him by making growling or barking noises.

He stopped his ears to their cries, aware only of Arron's words, and of the promise they seemed to contain:

It is our dearest wish to turn none from our door.

Someone older, wiser, might have seen in those words a polite rejection; but at fourteen, and with no experience of the greater world, he took them at their face value. For him, they were close to an open invitation. *None*, that was the word Arron had used—Boy had heard him distinctly—not a few or a handful, but *none*. Which meant—which *had* to mean—that nobody would be excluded, not even …

He paused in midthought. But why in fact should he go there? For what purpose? What awaited him in that distant place, and what exactly did he seek in the house of the rain-makers?

What …?

His footsteps had carried him high into the hills by the time he posed that question. The answer, when it came, was like a beam of bright light that made everything clear: his mysterious past, his future, his entire life.

Yes! he thought, as he ran back down through the slackening rain, Girl leaping along at his side. Yes! Here at last was the meaning of it all: the thing that had awaited him through his long years as an orphan and an outcast.

He reached the village, breathless, and went straight to Magda.

"You said … I special … yes?" he panted happily.

She wiped her hands on her dress and straightened from her work. "Yes, it's what I've always said. I knew it the moment I set eyes on you."

He nodded, eyes sparkling, raindrops falling like diamonds from his wet hair. "You right … I special … but now … know why."

She looked at him, curious. "Why is that?"

"You want … know?" He threw back his head in excited

laughter. "'Cause I ... I go Delta ... I find shaman ... I ..."

"You what?"

He grew suddenly serious, his young face hinting at how he would look in years to come. "I learn ... like ... like ... What Joel call ...? Like appren'ice. I learn ... everything. One day ... I shaman too."

She put both hands to her heart, as if in shock. "This is silly talk," she said in a whisper. "To become a shaman, a true rainmaker ... that's for great folk. Not for the likes of us."

"One day ... I great folk," he answered readily.

"Delta then," she went on. "It's too far away. You'd never get there. And even if you did, how would you live? Who would watch over you?"

"Girl ... she watch," was the reply.

"But you're too young!" she wailed at him. "What if I keep you here? If I refuse to let you go?"

He looked at her with eyes so fiercely dark that she flinched away.

"No keep," he said solemnly. "I go ... Delta. I go ... be shaman. For this ... I make promise." Here, he grasped the dog skull he wore and held it up for her to see. "I make promise ... for mother."

She knew then there was nothing more she could say.

PART III

| the youth |

11

The next morning dawned bright and clear, with no sign of rain. The riverbed remained dry. Yet there was now enough moisture in the soil for the people to begin planting, so most were in their gardens, hoeing and digging, when Boy set out.

Preparing for the journey had taken only a matter of minutes, because he wore most of what he owned. His other possessions—a handmade knife and spear, a rabbit-skin cloak, some strips of dried meat—he bundled together and slung across his back. With Girl almost stepping on his heels, he had hopes of leaving the village unnoticed; but Magda was on the lookout for his departure and, abandoning her work, she waylaid him down by the riverbank.

She also carried a small parcel of cornbread left over from the evening meal. Her face wet with tears, she pressed the food into his hands.

Embarrassed by her grief, he kissed her clumsily— aware, all at once, that he would miss her more than he had imagined.

"I ... come back ... soon," he muttered, telling her what he thought she wanted to hear. "I not go ... for always."

"Yes, you will," she sobbed. "The city will swallow you. We'll never see you here again."

He made as if to turn away, but stopped, unwilling to break the ties that bound him to this woman—the one person who had really cared for him over the years. Seeing how she bowed her head, meek and accepting even now, he felt a pang of regret. Because he knew she was right. They would probably never meet again after this. And he hated that idea. Hated it so much that, on the spur of the moment, he blurted out the first thought in his head.

"You come ... Delta too. Later ... maybe. You finish ... work for Phylo ... you follow. I ... I wait ... in city. Yes?"

He saw her hesitate, tempted by his offer, and immediately draw back, appalled by her moment of daring.

"How could I?" she mumbled through her tears. "I have no gold, no clothes to call my own ... nothing. I'd be a beggar in the city."

He looked at her worn dress and her bare feet, at her hair held in place by a string of twisted grass. It was true, though he had barely noticed it before: she possessed almost nothing. Not so much as a necklace or a hand-carved brooch. And again he acted on impulse. Easing the bear's tooth from his ear—the one she had given him soon after his arrival in the village—he pressed it into her work-hardened hand.

"You rich ... now ... same me," he said with childlike simplicity. "You bring ... Delta. We share ... yes?"

She half shook her head, half nodded, too fearful to decide; and he guessed then that she would never find the courage to leave.

"You come ... you bring," he repeated, nearly as upset as she was.

To the distant sound of thunder, his own eyes brimming with unshed tears, he loped off along the valley. He had not gone far when he heard a shrill cry from behind. Was it Magda? Or an eagle perhaps, screaming to its unfledged young? He looked back briefly, expecting her still to be there, but the valley was empty.

Sadly, he walked on, picking his way through the sparse growth that lined the riverbank. In times of plenty, the grass would have been lush underfoot, the stunted bushes heavy with leaves. Now the damp earth was almost bare, just a few half-withered sticks poking skyward. He cut one of these for a staff, and with Girl's presence to comfort him, he tried putting thoughts of loss from his mind. Magda had told him he was special, *that* was what he must cling to, not this strange emptiness he felt.

In this determined frame of mind, he pressed forward, following the path of the vanished river. Thanks to the food he carried, there was no immediate need to stop and hunt, so he and Girl made good time for the first few days. But on the morning of the fourth day, they woke up hungry. Boy had finished the cornbread on the previous evening; the last of the dried meat he had tossed to Girl, who had bolted it down and whined for more. Their only option was to search out fresh supplies.

They had reached a much flatter, hotter part of the country. Here, there were no foothills to hunt in, just featureless desert which stretched away in all directions. The one possible hunting ground was the riverbed itself. Like a great serpent, it meandered lazily through the land, twisting and turning endlessly. Sooner or later, every living thing—whether bird or beast—was drawn to it.

The problem, in such open terrain, was how to ambush their prey, and Boy decided on the simplest kind of trap. Having sniffed out water, he and Girl dug a shallow well and allowed it to fill. Then they hid behind some boulders a short distance downwind.

The scent of water soon had its effect. First, a sharp-quilled porcupine ambled across the sand; followed soon afterwards by a hare and a group of tiny desert gazelles. At the sight of the gazelles, Girl needed no instruction. Ears flat, she circled around and came at them from upwind, driving them straight toward Boy ...

Minutes later, he was gutting one of the tiny carcasses. The innards he threw to Girl; the haunches he roasted over a freshly laid fire of dry reeds. But if the scent of water was a sure lure, so was the smell of cooking meat. And on this occasion it attracted a dangerous predator—perhaps the most deadly of all.

Boy had just finished eating, and was packing up the rest of the meat—rolling it in the gazelle skin—when he heard an unusual whistling sound. A bird? A lizard? Girl, asleep until then, raised her head from the dry sand and listened. Whatever it was, it seemed to alarm her, because she rose stealthily to her feet, ready to slink off. Boy soon joined her, the pair of them moving noiselessly back to the refuge of the boulders.

They found more than good cover there. Caught in their own trap, they were suddenly surrounded by black-clad human figures. One hurled a weighted rope that coiled about Girl's legs and brought her down. Another tossed a fine-meshed net that settled over Boy like the clinging strands of a giant spider's web. The more he struggled against those strands, the more he became entangled. Until at last the largest of the figures threw him to the ground and fell upon him, knees first, crushing the air from his body.

He blacked out for a while. When he came to, his hands were bound and he was sitting propped against a boulder. Girl, still unconscious, lay sprawled on the sand some distance away, blood snaking from one nostril.

"I see our young hunter is awake," he heard someone say, and he turned to where his attackers were gathered about the fire.

The burliest of them—the man who had knocked him senseless—rose from the fire, a piece of half-cooked meat in one hand, and ambled over. He had pulled aside his head-dress, to reveal a less than young face framed by hair and beard nearly as black as his robes. Beyond his broad shoulders, Boy could see that the others were mostly children—boys and girls of various ages. Only one was adult, a woman he took to be their mother.

So ... a family group. A fact that gave him a small lift of hope ... until the man spoke.

"You ready to die, boy?"

He shrugged, pretending not to understand, and the man knuckled him across the mouth. He winced, and tasted his own blood.

"You ready?" the man repeated. "Because that's the rule in these parts. You steal someone's hunting ground, and you pay with your life."

"I ... I stranger," he explained through swollen lips. "I no ... steal."

"Oh, but you did," the man corrected him sharply. "And we judge people by their actions around here. Not by what they know or don't know."

"Finish him, Da," a childish voice called out.

The woman added: "You can see to the dog as well while you're about it."

A knife had appeared in the man's hand. He ran his tongue along its edge, as though testing it, and Boy let out a small sob of dread. He couldn't help himself. More than anything else, he wanted to close his eyes; to shut out the sight of what must happen next. But what about after that? What about Girl? There might still be time for *her* to save herself; to scamper away, if only he could rouse her.

In what Boy believed were the last few seconds of his

life, he turned to Girl and made a series of whimpering cries. They *did* rouse her to some extent, but not enough. She opened her eyes, staggered groggily to her feet, and was brought down again, by the same weighted rope as before.

The rest of the family gathered about her, laughing.

"What shall we do with her, Da? Shall we finish her off?"

"No, wait a minute." The man looked from Boy to the dog with a puzzled frown. "There's something going on here. Did you hear how he called to her? Like he could speak her tongue or something."

"You saying he's an animal?" the woman asked.

"Maybe. There's one sure way to find out."

Slowly, deliberately, he pressed the knife to Boy's throat. The point punctured the skin, and Boy, in blind panic, reverted to his early training. Baring his teeth, he snapped and snarled, braving the knife in an effort to bite the man's hand.

The woman came and crouched beside her husband, who eased the pressure on the knife and rocked back onto his heels.

"Did you see that?" he said in amazement. "When you get him cornered, he acts like a hound."

"What difference does that make?" the wife demanded.

"None maybe. Then again, maybe a lot." He pulled at his whiskers and gazed thoughtfully across the riverbed. "That well there, for instance," he went on, jerking a thumb over his shoulder. "It's not deep, and yet it's full of water. He dug it in just the right spot. How d'you reckon he managed that?"

"The dog could have sniffed it out for him."

"We've tried dogs. You know what they're like. They

sniff water all over the place, but a lot of it's too deep to find."

"So what are you saying? That he's a boy with a dog's instincts?"

"He barks and bites like a dog, doesn't he? He talks their lingo. Well, maybe he's also got their sense of smell. And something more besides. Some human know-how." The man lurched to his feet. "Here, let's see how he goes second time round."

Grabbing Boy by the hair, he hauled him upright. "You find me more water—surface water like that well over there—and you live. Understand?"

Boy was about to nod when he glimpsed Girl from the corner of his eye and thought better of it. She lay half crushed into the sand, struggling to breathe under the weight of two hefty children.

"Dog ... she live ... too," he replied softly.

The man brought his face close to Boy's. "You bargaining with me?"

He refused to meet the man's eyes, remembering his dog training. "Both live ... we find ... plenty water. Both ..."

The man considered the idea before nodding. "Right, it's a deal."

Pulling a rope from an inner pocket, he fashioned one end into a hangman's noose and slipped it over Boy's head. A second rope was produced by his wife, for Girl. When both nooses were in place, the man jerked them tight, warning his captives what to expect if they tried to run off.

"Now find me some water," he said gruffly.

Easing the tension in the rope with one hand, Boy set off along the riverbed, Girl a pace or two to his left, her nose nearly touching the ground. She was the first to stop: head down, she barked once and made a digging motion with her front paws. Boy went to the spot and sniffed. Then sniffed again.

"No … too deep … this one," he said.

They were off again, Boy tugging gently at the rope because he could sense something up ahead. He and Girl reached the place together. It was a slight depression in the sand, as bone dry as the rest of the riverbed, but they both stopped and sniffed eagerly.

"This … good well," Boy said, pointing. "You … dig."

"No, *you* dig," the man corrected him, and allowed a little more slack in the rope. "For your sake, I hope you're right."

Down on his knees, Boy began scooping away the sand. Barely half a meter from the surface, he felt the touch of cool water on his fingers; then smelled the fresh sweetness of it as it pushed up from below and rapidly filled the hole.

"Hell!" the man swore, and laughed aloud. "Will you look at that! He did it again. He chose just the right spot." He turned happily to his wife. "You know what this means, don't you? With these two to find for us, we'll never go thirsty again."

That one word, "never," made Boy leap to his feet and pull the rope taut.

"You say … free … if … if … find water."

"No, not free," the man corrected him again. "I said you'd live. You and the dog both. *Live*, nothing else, so don't go expecting too much."

"But … but …!"

His protest was choked off by a vicious tug that left him gasping and retching. Before he could regain his breath, he and Girl were urged forward, the whole group tramping off down the riverbed.

An hour's walking brought them to a bend in the river

bordered on one bank by a low hill, or what passed for a hill in this desert wasteland. In reality, it was not much more than a heaped jumble of rocks and silt, thrown up by repeated floods. At its highest point stood a ramshackle structure of wood and clay, with ancient palm fronds for a roof.

"You'll be calling this home for a while," the man said when they reached it.

Thinking he was being told to go inside, Boy reached for the door flap, and was instantly dragged backwards, but with such force that the rope bit into his neck and choked off his breath entirely. Lying half conscious on the sand, gasping for air, he was dimly aware of Girl barking somewhere in the background. Then the barking was replaced by a whimpering cry, and after that, silence.

Someone must have loosened the rope, because when he recovered minutes later, he found he was breathing freely again. He and Girl had been tied to one of the sturdy timber posts that held up the roof of the house. Behind them, inside the house, the family was talking and laughing together. If he listened hard, he could hear another, fainter noise: a kind of swishing sound, of something dry and smooth rubbing against itself.

He had to wait to discover the source of that sound. First, early in the afternoon, he and Girl were led out to find water close to the house. They were taken this time by the children, who proved much harsher than their parents. Every few minutes, they would tug at the ropes for the fun of it. Even when Boy found the well they were hoping for, less than a hundred paces from the hillock, they showed no mercy.

"Look at them," the two boys giggled, watching with delight as their captives fought for breath.

When Boy snapped and snarled in response, the girls beat him into submission with the sticks they carried.

Bruised and breathless, he dragged his way back up the hill, where the parents awaited them ... and so did the cage!

It was made partly from sticks that had been bound together to form a box; and partly from lengths of thickly plaited reeds which crisscrossed each other like bars. Seeing the plaited reeds, Boy understood the meaning of the earlier swishing sound. He also understood, with a sinking heart, that he and Girl were here to stay. For the reeds and the corner bindings looked strong. It would take more than a long night of gnawing for Girl to bite through them.

He was given little time to consider this dismal truth. As he strained back, the wife lifted the hinged flap of their cage. He tried to resist, but a fresh tug on the rope reduced him to helplessness; while a leather-shod foot kicked him and Girl roughly through the opening.

The children—the ones he came to hate most—pressed their faces to the reed bars.

"The dogs are in their kennel," they sang in shrill voices, chanting it over and over until he sank down in exhaustion and slept.

12

At the end of a week, Boy could not have said what he found harder to bear: the captivity, or the endless torment. Though for him, perhaps, the very worst moment was when the wife reached through the bars one day and snatched off his necklaces.

"What's all this rubbish you wear?" she asked idly.

Boy had never known life without the comforting feel of his precious charms. Deprived of them, he felt naked, cruelly exposed to the world of mankind.

"Give ...," he pleaded, clutching at the reed bars. "Give ... please."

The man took the necklaces from her and also inspected them. "Nothing here of value," he commented, and tossed them far from the house, where they rolled off down the hillside.

"No ...!" Boy shrieked, and hurled himself against the cage. "Give ...! Give ...!"

When he failed to calm down, the man hauled him from the cage and beat him. Yet that did no good either. He merely reverted to his dog self, snarling and biting until the tightened noose did its usual work.

He continued to act like a maddened dog when he was again taken from his cage hours later, this time to hunt out a fresh well. Instead of submitting to the lead, he fought it desperately, and had to be dragged down to the riverbed. There he bit the rope, the man's hand, anything he could reach. A second beating only made him more savage. Frothing at the mouth, he wound himself about the rope in an attempt to reach the man's throat; and when that failed, he rushed in and snapped at his heels.

The next two days followed the same pattern of attacks and beatings. His back became bruised and discolored; his neck grew raw from the noose; his hands bled from the hours he spent tugging at the bars. Nor did the nights make any difference to him. He fought on, howling at the stars, his dismal cries keeping the whole family awake.

In the end, it was the howling that defeated his captors. Late one afternoon, faced with the prospect of another sleepless night, the man rescued the necklaces from down the slope and tossed them into the cage.

"Here, you can have your trash if you want it," he muttered, his face flushed with resentment. "It's no damn use to me."

Boy fell upon his charms with a sob of relief and hugged them to his chest. Holding them there, warm and safe, he felt like someone emerging from a dark place. As the rage and desperation cleared from his mind, he ceased to snarl and howl and froth at the mouth. Gradually, he grew calm, more reasonable, more human again.

He had learned something about himself, however. Deep inside, he was not so very different from the wild packs after all. He too could be mindless and cruel, ready to bite and maim anything within reach. Like them, a part of himself remained truly savage. At heart, he was still wild, untamed, a creature who dwelt beyond reason.

And Girl? His faithful friend? Was this true of her as well?

That night, curled up in one corner of the cage, he looked

across at her sleeping form. With her snouted face softened by the moonlight, she appeared harmless enough. A trusted companion, tame since birth. Then she twitched in response to a dream; her snout wrinkled, revealing the gleam of teeth within; a low rumble issued from her throat. And he knew that somewhere inside, she was as savage as himself. Or as their captors, come to that, who treated them both so cruelly.

The next day, he submitted once again. When the man took them from the cage, he trotted along at Girl's side and dutifully hunted out a fresh well. He was just as docile hours later, when the children poked at him through the bars of the cage or reached in and tugged his hair. Although he growled a warning, he wasn't about to bite.

"I see the boy's learning at last," the man remarked in passing.

In part that was true, but not as the man had meant it. Boy *was* learning: to be watchful; to bide his time; to await the right opportunity. He may have been acting the part of a dog, but secretly he had never been more human.

His chance came on a searingly hot afternoon. The children had set up a target and were pegging at it with what they called their "knives"—jagged slivers of stone bound at one end with more of the plaited reed. Overcome by the heat, they soon gave up their game and trooped indoors to sleep, leaving the knives behind. The parents were also resting by then, and were likely to remain so for a while. At the very least, Boy had an hour in which to work.

The task before him was somehow to reach the knives. Most were stuck in the target, but one had glanced off and lay in the dirt several paces from the cage. What he needed was a length of cord that he could loop into a type of lasso. His own restraining rope was always kept indoors, so that was no help; and there was nothing of any use within arm's reach. Which left only the cage itself … his eyes settling at once on the plaited reed bars.

Several of the bars, he noticed, were looking frayed and worn, from the way he had attacked them in previous days. Carefully, he began picking at some of the loose fibrous strands, working them free, and soon he had enough to twist into a short string. He picked at others, lengthening the string as he went.

Within an hour the string itself reached almost to the knife, though it lacked a loop. He spent more time adding to it, and still it wasn't quite long enough. He was well into the second hour by then. Already he could hear movement from inside the house! He checked the bars once more, for loose strands, but most had been picked clean. Frantically, he searched the rest of the cage … his eye settling now on Girl's string collar, with its gleaming eye-tooth. *That* cord was too short, whereas the necklaces around his *own* neck …!

He lifted one clear. It was the string that held the most precious relic of them all: his mother's skull. Everything within him rebelled against the idea of using it. Equally, he hated the thought of enduring this captivity a moment longer than he had to. And here was an opportunity that he could not—*must not*—let slip by.

Hastily, he slid the skull off its cord, fashioned the cord into a simple noose, and tied it to the longer string. As he tossed it toward the knife—and missed!—he was aware of further movement in the house: of a child coughing and people talking quietly among themselves, the way they do soon after waking. Another toss … and another miss. A third attempt—with footsteps sounding from inside—and this time the noose found its mark. A gentle pull on the string, to close the noose around the hilt, and he was dragging the knife toward him.

He had only a few seconds left—the man's even tread telling him that. Shoving the knife deep into his tangled hair, he rethreaded the skull, snapped off the original cord, and looped it back over his head. The rest of the string he rolled into a ball that he wedged inside the empty skull.

Except for a slick of sweat on Boy's forehead, nothing looked amiss when the man emerged through the door flap moments later.

"Hunting time," he announced, and dropped rope leads into the cage for his captives to wear. "Let's see if you can use those noses of yours to sniff out game as well as water."

Releasing the hinged side of the cage—which was secured by two stout ropes tied to a roof pole—he led them out into the waning heat of the day. Although the sun was quite low, the air still shimmered in the near distance, creating an illusion of pools and lakes, and even shadowy groves.

"See how this country can fool you," the man said, pointing to the gleaming pools. "It's forever playing tricks on the eyes. On the ears too sometimes, because sounds can come at you from all directions at once in open country like this. The only thing you can really trust here is your nose—which is where you two come in." And he tugged at their leads, guiding them down to the riverbed.

Since his capture, Boy had picked out a series of wells that reached far downriver. Most of these were not for the use of the family, but to lure game, and with Girl loping ahead, they set out to inspect them.

Great care was necessary in the approach to each well. They made sure the wind was in their faces, and they took advantage of any cover. Yet despite their care, they drew a blank time and again. It was not until they neared the final well that Boy detected something. In the last of the sunlight, the riverbed streaked with evening shadows, he glimpsed a dark speck that seemed to waver and dip. It could have been an animal, a human, or simply a trick of the light, because Boy blinked once, and it vanished.

"What is it?" the man whispered.

Boy motioned for him to stay quiet, and then led the way over to a small stand of saltbush. From there, they had a clear view of the brimming well, which was ringed with tiny gazelles. Most were busy drinking, but one, a lookout, had stationed itself on a raised knoll about thirty paces to their left. It would have spotted the hunters instantly but for the setting sun, which blinded it when it gazed in their direction.

Was this the creature he had glimpsed earlier, Boy wondered? It *had* to be, because there was nothing else around, though to his eyes it looked too small. Also too delicate, with its gracefully curved horns and twitching nostrils. Not that any of this mattered in the here and now. The important thing was to restrain Girl and give the man a chance to take aim with his bow.

Close to Boy's ear, there was a sharp twang. Like a puppet worked by invisible strings, the gazelle leaped and stumbled … leaped again … and fell dead upon the sand.

The rest of the herd had vanished when they reached the carcass, Girl barking excitedly. Boy, by contrast, always felt sad after a kill. He killed in order to eat, like everyone else, but still it left him with a sense of loss. This present hunt was no exception, and while the man went about the grisly business of gutting and skinning, he sat slightly apart, silent and thoughtful.

It was while he was sitting there, pondering the gazelle's last moments, that something else caught his attention. Not this time a speck of movement against the evening landscape, but a sound. A kind of half cry. But from where? Behind him perhaps? He spun around and, like the gazelle, was blinded by the setting sun, which hovered on the horizon. The same sound reached him again, from a little to the right of the sun now. He tried to move toward it, only to be pulled up sharply by the rope.

"What's bothering you?" the man demanded, glancing up from his bloody work.

Boy touched his ear and pointed outward, but the man merely laughed.

"Didn't I tell you how it is in these parts? Sounds coming from everywhere; visions of things that don't exist." He laughed again. "Like I said, your nose is the one thing you can trust."

But when Boy sniffed the wind, that was no use either, because the air was too rank with the scent of blood. In any case, the sounds had stopped, the whole valley suddenly plunged into deep shadow as the sun dipped beneath the horizon.

In the eerie silence that occurs just before night, the man finished his work and cleaned his hands in a patch of coarse sand. "Yes, a hell of a place," he observed moodily. "Haunted, if the truth be told, by spirits of the dead."

Then he lifted the butchered carcass onto Boy's shoulders and they headed back, for what Boy hoped would be his last night of captivity.

13

They ate well that night, which was lucky for Boy on two counts: he knew the family would sleep extra soundly; and he, once free, would not have to stop and hunt for at least two days. Three, perhaps, if he pushed himself.

The main challenge, however, was to break out of the cage, and he waited impatiently for the family to go to bed. The lamp was doused at last; the family members settled one by one; and soon he could hear the snores and sighs that signaled deep sleep.

Only then did he pull the knife from its hiding place in his tangled hair. It was a crude thing, but reasonably sharp along its jagged edge. By the light of the moon, he considered where to begin: whether to cut through the bars; or to try and sever the twin ropes that held the side of the cage closed. The bars were thinner, but he would need to cut more of them. In fact, cutting a hole big enough to squirm through might take more time than he had. The twin ropes, on the other hand, looked too thick and tough for his simple blade.

Reaching through the bars, he tried the knife on the nearer of the ropes. The rough fibers parted more readily than he'd expected, and he began sawing away in earnest. Little by little, with the moon climbing ever higher, he hacked through the plaited cords, until the first of the ropes parted—its loose end swinging back against the roof-pole where it was tied. The second rope took longer to cut, because his knife was growing blunt; but around midnight, that also parted and swung free.

Cautioning Girl to remain silent, he lowered the side of the cage and crawled out. Inside the house, the family slept on, and Boy was about to steal away, thankful to be free, when he had second thoughts. These people had used him cruelly, depriving him of freedom, dignity, everything. So why shouldn't he take something from them in turn, as payment?

The man's bow and quiver of arrows hung from the eaves, and he slung them both across his shoulder. The rest of the meat hung nearby, left there to cure, and he took that too, plus his rabbit-skin cloak, which had been used as a doormat. Having rolled them together, he tied the bundle with the twin ropes he had cut from the cage, and crept off into the night.

All the way down the shallow slope, he was ready for the man's voice to cry out from behind; or for one of the weighted cords, thrown so expertly by the children, to come whirling after him. But he and Girl reached the riverbed undetected. Apart from the shrill chirrup of insects, there wasn't a sound. The first of the wells glittered in the moon-light and, pausing just long enough to drink their fill, they set off at a loping run.

The first hour took them past most of the wells they had dug. At the final well, Boy could not resist stopping for a while to listen. Yes, that sound again! The same moaning cry as before, more unnerving here in the depths of the night. Could it really be the ghost of some departed spirit, as the man had suggested? He shivered at the thought, and would have run on, but for Girl.

She was standing stock-still, her ears and ruff both

raised, her eyes fixed on the darkness. She refused to budge even when he called to her, eager to put this haunted place behind them.

"What … you see?" he muttered, and waited for her answering growl.

Instead, she wagged her tail and made a small welcoming noise. Straightaway, that other sound, somewhere out in the dark, seemed to answer. And she barked, joyously, and barked again.

"Hush!" he cautioned her, and clamped both hands around her muzzle.

He could feel her struggling against him. Could it be that these spirits were friendly? As she whined and strained, he released her and watched as she galloped off and stopped beside some bushes in a spray of sand.

What was she doing over there? He lowered his bundled cloak to the ground; fitted an arrow to the bow and crept forward. High above, the moon slid behind the clouds. When it reappeared, flooding the valley with silver light, he saw that she was licking at something in the shadow of the bushes. Licking …? He tiptoed a little nearer. He could see more now: a flutter of coarse cloth; what appeared to be a raised hand, reaching feebly up to Girl; a face half-hidden by a shock of steel-gray hair …

The truth came to him in a rush. With a welcoming cry of his own, he ran over and dropped to his knees in the sand.

"Magda …!" he burst out happily.

She tried to answer, but was too weak. She was also feverish. Her face and arms were slick with sweat, her forehead hot to the touch.

He bent closer and whispered anxiously: "Why … you sick?"

Although she could not answer directly, he saw her eyes

flick toward the woven bag beside her head. Inside, wrapped in a spare cotton shift, he found a small heap of fawn-colored lichen, of the kind that grows on the undersides of rotting wood.

"You ... eat?" he asked.

The moment she nodded, he guessed the rest. How, days out from the village, her food exhausted, she had collected these to stave off hunger. *This* was the result!

He threw the lichen aside in disgust and barked a warning to Girl when she went to sniff at it. He could not afford another sick friend. Their plight was desperate enough already. For even if Magda survived—and he prayed fervently that she would—she would need days to recover. Days! Whereas the family was only an hour behind. Come dawn, or perhaps sooner, they would find the cage empty and begin the hunt.

To stay there with Magda meant recapture; to abandon her was unthinkable. That left one possible middle path—to take her with him—and to do that he would need some form of litter or stretcher, to help him bear the weight.

Before succumbing to the fever, Magda had taken refuge beneath one of the many clumps of saltbush that dotted this part of the riverbed. These bushes, though leafless from the drought, had developed sturdy stems in order to withstand occasional floods. Using the knife and his own weight, he broke off two of the thicker stems. Stripped of twigs, these became the sides of his litter. A third stem, lashed in place with a piece of rope, served as a crosspiece to keep them apart; while his cloak, also lashed in place, formed the soft inner bed. The remaining rope, tied to the upper end of the litter and padded with Magda's spare shift, became a halter or yoke that would fit comfortably across his shoulders.

The work once complete, he first went to fetch Magda

some water from the well—in his own mouth, because he had no cup. But on the point of rolling her gently onto the litter, he foresaw a problem. Dragged along behind, the two ends of the litter would leave deep grooves in the sand, a clear sign that the family could follow with ease. Burdened only by their weapons, and traveling at three times his speed, they would overhaul him within hours. In all likelihood, he would be fighting them off before noon the next day.

No, there had to be an alternative, one that would throw the family off the scent. Skilled in the ways of the wild, he pictured it to himself immediately ... and hesitated.

Ever since his days with Joel, he had had a horror of being treated as a beast of burden. He had vowed never to suffer it again. Except this was Magda! It was different. Putting aside his vow, he hauled her onto his shoulders and tottered away from the riverbed, out into the desert.

A fully grown woman was a huge weight for a four-teen-year-old boy, but he staggered along until the ground became hard and stony underfoot. Leaving her there, he went back for the litter, and this time used a leafy branch to wipe out all his tracks. Now the family could follow him to the final well, and there the trail would end. With luck, the man might think he had been spirited away by the same ghostly presence that had moaned at them on the previous evening.

Boy, meanwhile, was well clear of the riverbed. Loading Magda onto the litter, he set his shoulders to the yoke and strained forward. Here in the desert, the stones bruised his heels; but the ground, baked hard by the sun, revealed only the faintest of trails.

For the rest of the night and far into the day, he labored on. The mounting heat defeated him at last. After erecting a simple shelter, from cactus and desert scrub, he returned to the riverbed and sniffed out a well. Three times he made the trip from well to shelter, using a scrap of leather from the cloak to hold water within his cupped hands. He almost didn't make a fourth trip, he was so tired, but knew he could not rest yet. Half walking, half crawling, he went back to fill in the well and wipe away his tracks once again. That done, he fell into a dead sleep that lasted until evening.

Magda was much better when he awoke—able to speak and sit up. Seeing how tired he looked, and how stiffly he rose from the sand, she tried persuading him to camp there awhile longer. Even when he explained about the family, she was not convinced of the need to press on.

"We're well ahead by now," she said. "If we rest tonight, I'll probably be able to walk a little by morning. We'll soon make up the time we've lost."

She nearly won him over. But soon after dark, on his second visit to the reopened well, he spotted telltale specks of black far off in the moonlight. The family! They were spread out from bank to bank, searching for signs.

Hastily, he refilled the well and threw dry sand over the top to hide the recent digging. Then, using the low bank as a shield, he hurried back to camp, wiping out his tracks as he went.

They were soon on their way, though this night proved harder than the first. Long before dawn, he began stumbling with fatigue; and at first light, he toppled face down in the sand.

Magda awoke him an hour later. "We need shelter from the heat," she said, "and water."

She had risen shakily from the litter, and together, half-supporting each other, they limped down to the river. With Girl's help, it took him only minutes to detect an underlying stream, and a few minutes more to dig a shallow well.

Gratefully, he and Magda plunged their heads into the cool water, relishing the sweetness of it.

When they rose, dripping, he noticed how still Girl was standing. How tense and alert. He followed the direction of her gaze and spotted them ... the family again! They were farther upstream, and it was obvious that they had sighted their prey, because they were running full tilt in his direction. If he listened hard, he could already hear their wild cries.

There was barely time to scramble back to the partial cover of the riverbank. Unslinging his bow, he fitted an arrow to the string. He had never used a bow before, and it felt clumsy in his hands, but anything was better than giving up without a fight. Picking out the lead figure—the man!—he took careful aim and let fly.

That first arrow fell well short of its target. The second flew past the man's head. Boy had the range now, and was straining at the bow for the third time, when he felt Magda's hand on his shoulder.

"There are too many," she said softly. "They'll kill you in the end."

He was convinced they would kill him anyway, and he took aim yet again—only to have her snatch the arrow from the string and snap it in two.

"Have some sense!" she hissed. "They'll treat us worse if you hit one!"

He looked bleakly at her. He longed to explain what it had been like in the cage. The way it had reduced him to the level of a wild dog. The hopelessness he had felt. But now was not the time for such talk. Grim-faced, he turned toward the oncoming family ... and watched in amazement as they suddenly slithered to a halt on the far side of the well. It was as if they had encountered an invisible barrier they were unable to cross. They continued to shout and shake their weapons, but that was all.

"What can be holding them there?" Magda asked in a frightened whisper.

"They have reached the limit of their hunting grounds," a voice answered.

Girl let out a frightened yelp. Boy and Magda whirled around, to find themselves confronted by another group of black-clad figures.

The person who had spoken—a middle-aged woman and the leader—stepped forward and plucked the bow from Boy's hands. "No one employs a weapon on this portion of the river except us," she cautioned him. "That is why our neighbors cannot approach. These are our grounds and ours alone. They can bargain for you, but they cannot enter our land and take you by force."

Magda clutched at the woman's hand. "You will save us?"

The woman gave a sly smile. "I did not say that exactly, though of course rescue is always possible at a price."

"A *price*?" Magda wailed. "But we have no gold! Nothing of any value to trade with!"

The woman's smile was replaced by a sterner expression. "Then perhaps our neighbors are ready to trade. Are you worth gold to them, do you think? Shall we ask?"

She paused, awaiting an answer, and Boy, having recovered from his initial surprise, looked into her face. He glimpsed guile there, and greed, but none of the cruelty he had seen in the faces of the family.

Pointing to himself, he said firmly, "I ... trade."

"Do you now?" She laughed and crooked an eyebrow at him. "I see only a naked boy, not yet a man, with nothing to call his own. If I'm not mistaken, even this bow, and those arrows, were stolen from my neighbor. So what can someone like you possibly offer us?"

He indicated the well, farther out on the sand. "This one … I make. You like … I dig … two more … same like this."

"And in exchange?"

"Safe passage," Magda begged.

The woman gazed shrewdly at them both before walking over to inspect the well. When she returned, she muttered for a while to her followers, and then turned back to Boy.

"The well is good. You have tapped into a strong stream. Can you do that for us twice … no, three times more, down-river?"

He touched his nose and laughed. "I say … only two."

"Three is the price of safe passage."

"For three … you give food?"

"And sing our praises to the people in the next hunting ground?" Magda put in quickly.

It was the woman's turn to laugh.

"You drive a hard bargain for a pair of beggars. But yes, I agree to your conditions. The bargain is struck."

So saying, she spat on her hand and offered it to Boy. He looked at it in wonder for a moment. Apart from Magda, no one had ever treated him like this—as an equal—and he felt overwhelmed.

"Come, boy," the woman urged him. "This is an honest trade. Pledge yourself if you mean to deal fairly."

"Don't keep the mistress waiting," Magda added in a nervous whisper.

With a solemn face, he also spat into his hand. "We make … trade," he said, and returned her warm clasp.

14

With Magda and Girl's help, he easily kept to his bargain, and dug three good wells along a considerable stretch of riverbed. That done, they were passed on to the next group of "river guardians" as they called themselves; who in turn struck a bargain and passed them on to the next group.

In this way, they journeyed steadily downriver, Boy's fame as a water diviner growing as they progressed. All at once, he was a somebody out there on those sandy wastes; no longer a lowly dogboy, but a person of importance, looked up to by these simple hunting groups. While he dwelt among them, he was treated with genuine respect, each group offering small gifts over and above the agreed price of food and shelter and safe passage.

In the past, he had always slept on the ground. Now he was shown to beds of rushes that felt so soft they kept him wakeful for hours. Lying back, in what for him was untold luxury, he surveyed the passage of his young life—from dog, to boy, to slave, and then to this. How had it happened? He hadn't willed it—which surely meant that he was indeed special, as Magda claimed; not just any orphaned boy, but someone marked out for greater things.

As he thought these thoughts night after night, his confidence grew. He had been right to leave the village. He had not been vain or deluded when he had told Magda of his ambitions. His true destiny awaited him in Delta—he was convinced of it—in the house of Arron and Elvina. They would welcome him with open arms; accept him as their apprentice; teach him their mysteries. How could they do otherwise? Clearly, that was his fate. His present role as water diviner and digger of wells was just a first step. Delta would be the next. Until one day ...

Even when he slept, there was no escaping his brilliant future. It came to him in vivid dreams, in which he strode the world as a great shaman—a man like Arron, dressed in scarlet robes, with a fine house like those in the stories the villagers used to tell. Needy folk waited at his door, seeking his help; and a gesture from him made the rain fall, the river flow, the land turn lush and green.

Awake, he began to live out these dreams. To strut a little when he located a new well; to lift his chin and smooth his wild hair whenever his skills were praised. He even begged some clothing from one of the hunting groups, to cover his nakedness, and was given a threadbare black tunic that he wore proudly. As he stood beside his latest well, admiring his own reflection, he did not notice Magda watching him with concerned eyes; nor was he bothered by the way Girl sniffed suspiciously at this strange garment and slunk away.

Meanwhile, their long journey had brought them to where the snaking riverbed broadened and wound in upon itself like never before. Taking leave of their latest hunting group, they found that there was no one else to offer them safe passage. They had reached the end of the hunting grounds and now stood at the outer limits of the city.

They sighted it around the next bend, off in the hazy distance: an untidy cluster of mud-walled buildings, backed by the dense blue of the ocean and the lighter blue of the sky. It had been built close to where the river opened to the sea, and had been given its name because it occupied one bank of the delta. On the other bank, the desert stretched away into the haze.

As they drew nearer, they encountered the fringe dwellers: poor folk camped among the straggly palms that lined the banks. They also came upon the first of the wells: deep shafts that burrowed down into the sand. Some, long since dry, had begun to cave in. Others—the working wells—were guarded by armed men and had pyramids of palm-logs mounted above them to take the weight of the filled buckets.

A further hour's walking brought them almost level with the city. Here there were wells in plenty. Lines of camels, laden with leather water bags, traversed the riverbed. Tents had been erected all over the sand, and there was a general air of festivity. One man bawled out the price of his water. Another clinked the money in his purse and closed his well for the day. Yet another labored at raising water for a camel driver.

Wherever Boy looked, he saw people, more than he had ever imagined. Beggars, some of them horribly misshapen, pleaded for alms; supple young acrobats performed for a few copper coins; vendors, laden with baskets of bread or dates, staggered among the throng, in the hope of making a sale; and everywhere there were groups of ragged urchins, or of older, homeless youths.

One of the older groups sidled up behind Boy and Magda, dogging their heels as they threaded their way toward the city. When Girl turned threateningly, showing her teeth, they just laughed and drove her off with handfuls of sand.

One among them, a girl of about fifteen, in a fine straw hat, but otherwise dressed in rags, called out to Boy:

"Where are *you* off to in such a hurry?"

He gave her a proud glance, and bared his chest to show

her the charms he wore. "Me … I go … find rainmaker … great shaman."

He expected her to fall back in awe. Or at least to dip her head in respect, like the hunting groups he had dealt with. Instead, she bared her shoulders in mockery, and imitated his strange way of speaking.

"Me … I go … ask great shaman … to beat me."

Magda stopped and faced the girl. "Why ask him to beat you?" she demanded seriously.

It was one of the girl's companions who answered, a young lad of about the same age, with a wisp of beard already sprouting from the end of his chin.

"Look around you," he said, waving his hand at the dry riverbed. "It hasn't rained here for years. That's because there are no true rainmakers left. Only tricksters. Unless you go to them with gold in your hand, they beat you from their door. Or their followers do."

Boy also stopped and turned, his face twisted into a sneer of disbelief. "Arron … no trickster," he said coldly. "Shaman … only this."

"Arron?" the bearded youth took him up. "He's the worst of the lot. And that wife of his! The stupid dances she does. They're enough to scare the rain *away*."

While all the others were laughing, the girl in the straw hat pretended to be Elvina. Twirling around, she pointed to the spot between her feet and said in a singsong chant: "This place will I water with my tears. Here will the desert bloom again … Oh, but I forgot. First you must cross my palm with silver. Or better still, gold."

Boy, in a flash of protective anger, shoved the girl roughly to the ground. "Elvina dance … for people … not gold!" he shouted, and would have pushed at the bearded boy too if Magda had not held him back.

It was just as well that she did, because the laughter had stopped, their companions crowding in.

The girl rose and dusted the sand from her ragged clothes. "You don't believe us?" she said, staring past Magda to Boy. "Then go and find out for yourself. Try knocking at her door and see what happens."

"I go ... I try," Boy replied defiantly, and stalked off.

Magda caught up to him just as he was mounting the steep riverbank. Side by side, with Girl walking nervously in their shadow, they entered the maze of lanes that ran through the city. This first lane was crowded with a jostling throng made up of people, camels, donkeys pulling small carts, goats, pigs—even monkeys with jeweled hats that swung from the poles of wandering musicians. And the noise! In the confined space between the houses, it was deafening. People shouted or called to each other; donkeys brayed; iron-shod wheels screeched on worn flagstones; babies cried bitterly, wailing above the rest of the din.

Magda brought her face close to Boy's ear.

"Which way?" she yelled.

They had reached a star-shaped crossroads where five lanes met. Some were less crowded and noisy than others, but otherwise looked the same, all of them bounded by clay-built dwellings that showed only a blank wall to the outer world. It was cool in the shadow of these walls, the air heavy with a stomach-churning mixture of smells.

Receiving no answer from Boy, who stood there bewildered by it all, Magda turned to a passing stranger: an elderly man with a fuzz of gray beard and only one eye.

"Your pardon, sir," she said politely, "but can you direct us to the house of a rainmaker called Arron?"

The man fixed her with his remaining eye. "What business do you have with the likes of Arron?"

"My young friend here needs his help."

"Help? From Arron?" The man broke into explosive laughter. "Aah well," he managed at last, wiping a tear from his eye, "I suppose there's always a first time."

"A first time for what?" Magda demanded.

He waved her question aside. "If you're truly bent on seeing him, then take that lane back to the riverfront." He pointed to their right. "Once there, walk seaward until you can walk no farther. You'll find him near to river's end. The House of Rain, he calls it, though there are those who know it by other names."

"What other names …?" Magda began, but the man had gone.

Pushing through the crowd, they wound their way back to the riverbank and followed it toward the ocean. They soon came upon many fine houses out here, their raised terraces designed to catch the cooling sea breeze. The finest of them all stood on the farthermost point of land; and huddled beside it, as though basking in its reflected glory, was a much smaller dwelling. This house, like its larger neighbor, had a high surrounding wall and a magnificent gate, emblazoned with the shape of a shining raindrop.

"The House of Rain, the man called it," Magda said. "This must be the one."

A bronze bell hung beside the gate, and after a slight hesitation, Boy went over and pulled on its rope. There was a loud clang, followed by the sound of footsteps, and a slot opened in the gate. The upper portion of a face peered through, the eyes dull gray and hard.

In a voice to match the eyes, someone said: "We want no beggars here. If it's alms you seek, go to the marketplace and beg with the rest."

Magda tugged at Boy's tunic. "Come," she muttered,

"You have your answer."

Shaking her off, he pushed his face up to the slot. "Not beggar …!" he nearly shouted. "Arron … he tell me … you come … he no turn … from door. Arron … he say this."

"And I say *this*," the voice replied. "Our master has no dealings with beggars. So get away from this door while you're still in a fit state to walk."

The slot was about to slam shut when Boy shoved his fist into the opening.

"You tell … Arron … Elvina … you tell … Boy is come … from village."

There was cool laughter from inside the gate. "Oh, a village boy, that'll really get them excited. Any other important messages I should pass on while I'm about it?"

Boy nodded vigorously. "Yes … I come … learn make rain … be shaman … same like them."

More laughter. "Oh, they'll be glad to hear that too."

Satisfied, Boy withdrew his fist, and the eyes reappeared in the opening.

"Here's an idea," the voice said. "How about if you wait over there, by the sea wall? My master and mistress are busy right now. They'll come when they can, though it'll take a while. Quite a while, in fact. In the meantime, don't go ringing this bell, because they hate being pestered. Understand?"

"I understand … I wait," Boy said solemnly, and withdrew as far as the sea wall—a low sandstone coping that stood high above the dry delta.

A few hundred paces downstream, the high tides washed the delta mouth; but none reached into the riverbed itself, as though even the salt sea was wary of the land in these lean times. The ocean breeze was the only thing that ventured upriver, and Boy soon had need of it, because there was no cover beside the wall.

Once, palm trees in plenty had grown along the bank. Most had died in the past few years, and all had been uprooted and carted off for use at the wells. In the absence of these trees, the sun beat down on Boy's unprotected head with a fierceness he had never encountered in the upper valleys. Yet he had been told to wait, and that was what he was determined to do.

"Can't you see that they don't want you here?" Magda reasoned with him. "They probably don't remember that you exist. And that servant in there, he won't have told them anything, believe me. Why should he? These are grand folk, they're not interested in people like us."

To these and other arguments, Boy had just one reply: "Arron come ... I *know* this."

Unable to shake his confidence, she was soon driven off by the mounting heat, taking Girl with her.

"I'll be back later," she called, as they stumbled away down the road. "I'll fetch water if I can."

Left alone, Boy stood and faced the closed gate, steeling himself for a lengthy wait. By midday, he felt slightly sick from the heat; by midafternoon, he was so dizzy that the outlines of the House of Rain began to blur and melt into the surrounding sky. Half-delirious, he imagined the gate opening suddenly and two robed figures emerging.

"Welcome," Arron crooned.

"You are here at last," Elvina murmured, and draped a finely woven shawl around his scorched neck.

He could feel her tears upon his face; the cooling touch of her hands on his forehead; the gift of water on his tongue.

Could this really be happening, he wondered? He rubbed his eyes, and the two figures disappeared. He was alone again, with the closed gate and searing heat that threatened the whole world, himself included.

When Magda returned, at sundown, he was barely conscious. She had traded one of their small gifts—a woven brooch given to them by the "river guardians"—for a few dates and a pannikin of foul-smelling water. He sipped the water gratefully and revived enough to appreciate the cool of the evening.

Thinking he had learned his lesson, she urged him to rest awhile. "We can leave here in the morning," she said. "While it's still cool, we'll search for water. Sweet, fresh water, better than this, that we can sell in the market. In a week or two we can earn enough to …"

She noticed then that he wasn't really listening, and her heart sank. "You mean to stay here?"

"Arron come … Elvina come …," he answered stubbornly.

First thing the next morning, he resumed his vigil. And again, when the sun rose higher, Magda took Girl off to the markets, fearful that if she did not bring back water, Boy would die.

Throughout that second day, he stood facing the gate, as before. Except this time, in his delirium, he did not imagine it opening and robed figures emerging. Instead, he heard voices. Elvina's mostly.

"We are only testing you, that is all," she whispered. "We wish to see whether you are worthy."

"Worthy?" he queried aloud, through cracked lips.

"To be a great shaman."

His parched tongue moved sluggishly. "What … must … I do?"

He felt her cool breath upon his closed eyelids. "A true rainmaker must first learn to endure. To become like the sun-bruised land. Like the sun-washed sky. He must withstand all hardship, all suffering, and be unmoved by them.

Only when you have reached the end of endurance will the gate open to you—the greatest gate of them all."

He tried to moisten his lips, but his tongue was dry. "How ... long?" he managed.

"Three days and three nights," she murmured. "Throughout this time you must be steadfast. Unswayed by doubt. Will you do this? For Arron? For me? For the Great Father?"

"I will ... be ... steadfast," he croaked to the sunlit day, and felt the voices withdraw; felt the suffocating heat close in around him, almost stopping his breath.

Yet he understood now that he was merely being tested. The heat, the terrible thirst, his blistered lips and cheeks, these were not things of real importance. What mattered was the nature of the ordeal, and his determination to be found worthy. For he had come too far to admit failure. It had been a long road, he realized, one that had begun somewhere in the mountains, on the night of his birth. How much had he endured since then? So many dangers! So many hardships! So many humiliations! What were another three days compared to all of that? No, not as much as three days. Just one and a half days more and the long ordeal would be over: the great gate would open, as Elvina had promised, and he would step through. He would enter into the mystery of what it is to be a shaman ... a rainmaker ... a prince among men. He, too, would wear a red robe and speak to the skies.

"... to ... the ... skies," he muttered aloud.

He was still muttering it, over and over, in time to his swaying body, when Magda returned once more.

She was shocked by the state he was in: by his swollen tongue and the cracked skin of his cheeks. Tenderly, she lowered him to the ground; dribbled water between his lips;

chewed some of the bread and dates she had bought and pushed the soft mush into his mouth.

Again he revived and gazed up at her. "Two days ...," he whispered with a stiff smile.

"Yes, two days and no more," she said tearfully. "This is enough."

He did not answer her in words. He just held up three fingers of his right hand, and she guessed the rest.

"No," she pleaded. "Think of Girl. Think of me. Who will take care of us? Who will get us back to the village? Without you, we will be marooned here. The river guardians will never let us pass."

It occurred to him, dimly, that she was expecting him to die. Inwardly, he laughed at her foolishness. Did she understand nothing about the land and the skies above? He could no more die than they could, for soon he would be at one with them. A single day was all that stood between. Surely she could grasp that.

"One more ...," he breathed, "one more ...,"—and slept.

He awoke to the violent ringing of the bell. It was Magda, over by the gate, arguing with someone. He could hear her shouting from where he lay, then begging. Until the slot slammed shut, as he knew it must.

Painfully, he rose and faced the House of Rain once more. As the sun climbed higher, he heard a muffled farewell from Magda, followed by the departing shuffle of her bare feet and the click of Girl's claws. Yes, he thought, they have their road to walk; I have mine. His, though, was almost complete, and he held fast to that idea as the day progressed.

It was the hardest to bear of the three. No presences emerged from the gate; no voices whispered words of encouragement. He felt more alone than he ever had before. His mouth, too dry to speak, became dumb. His other senses closed to the blinding light and the burning rays. Shut in upon himself, he realized that this was what it must be like for the land: to have no human voice, no human sensations; to be mute before the onslaught of each day. The mercy of rain, of free-flowing water, was something that had to be earned. Like this ... Only thus could he learn those other tongues—of earth, air, fire, and water—and use them to plead for the skies to show pity.

Nobody showed *him* pity that day. He blacked out in the course of the afternoon; came to and staggered up, only to black out again. This same pattern repeated itself two ... three ... four times, and each time he found it more difficult to rise. Yet when the sun finally dipped toward the horizon, he was still more or less conscious, and still on his feet, though the gentle evening breeze caused him to sway like the palm fronds that had once flourished there.

He was muttering brokenly to himself when Magda arrived. She fed him a little water, but still he made no sense.

"What is it?" she asked, really alarmed now by his appearance.

"Same earth ... same sky ...," he moaned.

"What is? What's the same?"

But how could he tell her? The language of the earth, of the wind, was far beyond her understanding. It was meant for his ears alone; for him, and for no other human soul. If he shared it with anyone at all, it was with the sun ... and the sun had decided to sleep.

So did he, as never before. A deathly sleep that gradually gave way to a dream of running water and a cool palm grove. A group of young people, similar to those who had followed him days earlier, was seated beside the stream, some of them drinking from it. A girl among them, wearing a straw hat, leaped to her feet when she saw him, gratitude written clearly on her face. But he did not want her thanks, because this stream, these cool surrounds, were not meant for her and her companions.

He did his best to tell her that. To explain how all of this was his gift to … to … He fumbled for a name, a half-remembered face, but before he could recall them, he awoke. To a flush-pink dawn, the upper arc of the sun just showing above the horizon.

Groaning softly, he sat up and reached for the water bottle Magda had brought.

"Finish it," she said, and handed him a few moldy figs, plus the remains of the bread.

He wolfed these down too, and looked toward the gate. Full sunrise would signal the end of his three-day ordeal. When that happened, the gate would surely open. It *had* to! He rose expectantly, and took a few faltering steps forward as the world flooded with newborn light.

Still, the gate remained shut. Should he perhaps sound the bell? Is that what they were waiting for inside? For him to announce that his vigil was over? Complete? He cast an agonizing glance at Magda and saw only grief on her face.

"Come away," she said, and tugged at his arm. "It's over. They don't want you."

He yanked his arm free. How could she say such a thing? Shaking from the effort, he limped over to the bell and rang it; swung the clapper until the sound rang out across the delta.

"All right! All right!" a voice called from inside.

A slot opened; the same eyes appeared. Even he could see that they were not welcoming.

"Not you again, boy! Didn't I tell you not to ring? Didn't I?"

He did not attempt to answer. He could think of nothing to say, because in his weakened state none of this made any sense. As from a distance, he heard the bolts of the gate being drawn back. The gate itself swung open and a burly servant emerged—a squarely built man with a twisted mouth. He held a bamboo cane in his right hand.

"This is what happens to those who pester their betters!" he cried, striking repeatedly at Boy with the cane. "*This!* And *this*! And *this*!"

Curled up on the ground, arms raised against the onslaught, Boy clung to the last shreds of hope. For this to happen, he knew that he must have missed something; omitted some small but vital detail.

What could it be?

Then it came to him. Of course! His unfinished dream of the night before. And its promise of a gift.

15

With Magda's help, and with Girl trotting along behind, Boy managed to limp as far as the city. There, they bartered the last of their small gifts for food and water, and sat out the heat of the day in a tiny square, shadowed by mud dwellings.

Most of the time, Boy slept, slowly recovering some of his lost strength. And toward the end of the afternoon, he dreamed again of a palm grove with a cool stream running through it. The grove contained the same group of young people as before, and as in the earlier dream, he knew that this gift of running water was not meant for them. Or not for them alone.

He awoke with the dream still fresh in his mind, a smile on his sun-damaged face. For now he was doubly sure that in his eagerness to win entrance to the House of Rain, he had overlooked a vital detail. It was not enough to have proved himself worthy. Or to have endured three days of privation. He should also have shown that he was someone of *ability*; someone already skilled in the mysterious ways of water. Why, otherwise, should anyone open the gate to him? Well, there was one way of putting everything right, and he smiled again, remembering the clear message of the dream.

Seeing how happy he looked, Magda gave a puzzled frown.

"I thought you'd be sad after the way they treated you back there," she said. "Or at least disappointed. To come this far, only to be turned away empty-handed … that's hard."

To her surprise, he half agreed. "Yes … empty hand … bad. Full hand … better."

"Full …?" She failed to understand.

He cupped both palms together. "Water …," he explained, "for … for gift. I find … I take … next time."

"Next time?" She jumped up in alarm. "You're not going back there! You can't!"

"I … go back," he told her calmly. "I … ring bell … gate opens."

"But why? It didn't open last time. Like I said before, they're grand folk. They're not interested in us."

He shook his head and drew her down beside him. "I take … water … yes?" he began patiently. "Water for … House of Rain." He paused and laughed at how obvious it all seemed, amazed that he had not understood earlier. "Water is … how you say? … is … is *key* … to gate. They … take gift … they smell … fresh … sweet … Not same … other wells … pshaw!" He wrinkled his nose in disgust at the water they had bought that morning. "They smell … they say … welcome … They know … I shaman … one day."

Although she followed what he was saying, it did not bring her any joy.

"Listen to me," she said. "You've endured enough here. This is no place for us. It will only make us unhappy. Let's just find enough water for ourselves. Or trade some for gold if you want. Then let's go home."

"Gold … pshaw!" He wrinkled his nose once again. "I … no come … for gold. I … special … I come … be shaman … only this."

She knew him of old: how, once decided on a course of action, there was no dissuading him.

"Where will you find this fresh water?" she asked doubtfully. "You've seen the wells in the riverbed. Scores of them. Everyone's searching, and all they can find is this." She tipped their bottle and poured a little of the evil-smelling water into her palm. "Why should you be able to find anything better?"

"I ... look," he said confidently. "I ... find."

With a sigh, she gave in. "But if you don't, can we go home?"

He would have liked to reassure her, but couldn't.

"Village ... home ... for dogboy. Not for me. We stay ... we live ... big house. We ... happy. You see."

Would she? Stifling her doubts, she followed him through the late-afternoon streets to the river. The sun was close to setting, and out on the delta the business of the day was getting started. As they descended to the sandy bed, a group of familiar figures stepped from the crowd and confronted them.

Recalling their last encounter with these young people, Girl growled a warning and was hushed by Boy.

"We want no trouble," Magda told them. "We're just here to dig for water, like everyone else."

The girl in the straw hat nudged her companion. "Listen to this. They're water diviners now." Then directly to Boy: "What's the matter? You too proud to beg?"

"Haven't you heard?" the lad with the wispy beard broke in. "He tried begging outside the House of Rain."

"Judging by the looks of him, he didn't do too well."

"Yeah, the state he's in, he won't be up for much digging either."

The girl shrugged, finally stepping aside to let them pass. "He'll be wasting his time anyway. The only thing he'll find out there is his grave."

"I ... no find ... grave," Boy answered evenly. "I find ... water ... clean ... same wind ... same sky."

"Clean as the wind, eh?" The girl gave a good-natured chuckle. "If you could locate water like that, I'd dig the well myself."

"I find ... you dig," Boy took her up quickly.

"What's in it for us?" the bearded lad demanded.

Boy pointed to the bottles hanging from each of their belts. "I fill ... yes?"

The girl looked to her companion. "A bit of digging for a full bottle. What do you think?"

"Worth a try, maybe."

"Okay, it's a deal," she said, and offered Boy her hand. "Oh, my name's Kris, by the way, and this here's Jude. Don't worry about the rest, they're just hangers-on."

"I'm no hanger-on," someone said, and a little imp of a figure, with a hunched back and eyes blacker than the night, pushed his way forward. "People call me Petro. If you strike water and need bottles, jars, camels, anything at all, I'm the one you come to."

"We'll remember that," Magda said, amused by this curious creature.

Having completed their introductions, they set out across the sand as a group.

The sun was down now and, all across the delta, rush torches were flaring into life. By their smoky light, as well as by the lingering glow in the sky, Boy and Girl together led the way, searching between the various wells. In one place, Girl stopped and barked, but after scooping a little sand into his palm and sniffing at it, Boy shook his head and moved on. To a slight dip in the riverbed, where a previous well had been partly filled in. Again he sniffed at the sand; even pressed it to his tongue.

He grinned at his companions then, and indicated a spot less than a pace from the old well. "Plenty water ... you dig."

"Not me," Jude said, drawing back. "This well's played out. Anyone can see that."

Boy feather-touched the back of Kris's hand. "We make ... bargain ... yes?"

"Yes."

"Bargain say ... you dig ... yes?"

She grinned back at him. "Yeah, why not? Come on, Jude, let's give it a try."

Grumbling to himself, Jude knelt beside her and was about to start digging when Petro scuttled forward.

"Hey, wait a minute," he cried, stooping toward them. "You've got to rub my hump first, for luck."

But before they could touch his hunched back, Boy reached out and stopped them—his own childhood humiliations still too fresh in his mind.

"No ... need luck," he said. "Plenty water ... for sure."

"Here goes then," Kris said, and with Jude's help she began burrowing into the sand.

Within minutes, the work was interrupted by a gurgling sound. As they rocked back onto their heels, sweet-smelling water flooded into the hole.

"Great Father in the sky!" Jude gasped. "Can you believe that?"

Kris scooped some up and tasted it, then looked at Boy with new-found respect. "Was this first-time luck or what?"

"No luck ... I find ... every time."

Petro again scuttled forward. "Just tell me what you need. Big jars? Camels for carting them to market? I'll have them here within an hour."

"I … no take … to market."

Petro's dark eyes flashed in the light from a nearby torch. "You're not interested in selling this? Why not? A well of this quality, it's worth … I don't know … a whole bag of gold."

"I … no want … gold."

"So what *do* you want?" Kris asked quietly.

He motioned for Magda and Girl to satisfy their thirst, and did the same himself. Then he took the bottle Magda carried, washed it out several times, and filled it with fresh water.

"I … take … this."

"What about the rest?"

"For … you."

She caught at his hand before he could back away. "You promised only to fill our bottles. That was the bargain we struck."

"You fill … many times … maybe," he said with a laugh, and stepped free, out into the thickening dusk, with Magda and Girl close behind.

Magda did not question his decision—she had guessed he would do something like this. Nor did she wonder where they were headed, for she guessed that too. So that when he faltered, still weak from his ordeal, she took his weight upon her aging shoulders and led him out along the riverbank toward the ocean.

They reached the House of Rain in the last of the dusk. There was no lamp at the gate, but a light showed in the upper story of the house, visible above the wall. He stood gazing at it for a while, watching as the outline of a robed figure moved backwards and forward across it.

"Arron," he said at last, and went to the gate.

The clanging of the bell produced the usual result—the

same cold gray eyes gazing at them through the slit.

The same voice growled out: "Didn't you get enough last time?"

The bolts were drawn back and the gate swung open, but when the burly servant emerged, stick in hand, he was met by a splash of cool water that caught him across the mouth.

He put out his tongue and licked the drops from his upper lip. So sweet! He breathed in the smell of it. Sweeter still! Like a true citizen of Delta, where water was cherished above everything else, he threw aside his stick and bowed low.

"Forgive me, good sir," he said humbly. "I took you for someone else. Tell me what I can do for you this fine evening."

"Bring Arron … bring Elvina …," Boy said.

"My master and mistress? At once, good sir."

Another low bow and he was gone, leaving the gate wide open.

Boy was tempted to step through, but thought better of it. No, let them welcome him in, that was how it must happen.

Hearing raised voices from inside, and the clatter of hurrying footsteps, he readied himself for this, the most telling moment of his life. The moment when everything would change; when his days as a dogboy could be discarded forever.

"Have courage," Magda murmured in his ear.

He shrugged aside the warning, for he could see lamps being lit now. Held aloft by servants, they were used to usher out the great couple in their flowing robes.

Arron it was who reached the gate first. "You have water for sale? *Good* water?"

"Not sale … gift," Boy said, and handed him the nearly full bottle.

Arron sniffed at it and passed it to Elvina, who breathed in the sweet scent and felt for the purse at her waist.

"How much for the well?" she demanded.

"No trade …," he insisted. "This bottle … my gift … to you."

Elvina snatched a lamp from a servant and held it high, so as to see his face more clearly. "What do I want with a single bottle?" she rasped. "The whole well … that's another matter. Name a reasonable price and I'll take it."

"No trade …," he repeated. "Gift … only."

She advanced on him angrily. "Do you take me for a fool? Nobody gives things away in this city. Least of all good water. So name your price. Name it, damn you!"

Magda reached for Boy's hand, but it felt cold and lifeless. As did his face, which was fixed in an expression of shock.

"Tell her," she urged him.

A kind of shudder passed through his body, and an unforgiving glint showed in his eyes.

"You want … I make … bargain …?" he asked in a whisper. "Here … my price …" He took a deep breath. "I come … live in … House of Rain. I learn … be … great shaman … same like you. This only … my price."

Elvina turned toward her husband. "What's this nonsense he's talking? Can you make any sense of it?"

Arron took another of the lamps and moved to her side, effectively blocking the entrance. "As far as I can gather, he wants to become a shaman. He wants us to teach him."

Elvina burst into harsh laughter. "What? And all for a bottle of water?"

"This only … my price," Boy said again, in a firmer voice.

"Then here's mine," she flared back, and drawing a copper coin from her purse, she flung it at his feet. "That's for this one bottle. Either take it and be grateful, or tell me the whereabouts of the well, in which case I'll replace it with gold."

He stooped for the coin and gazed at it, turning it this way and that in the lamplight.

"What do you say?" Arron asked. "Is the well yours to sell or not?"

He looked up slowly. "Well not … for trade. Mine once … but no more. I … make gift … to beggars."

"To beggars!" Elvina snorted in disbelief. "This is just more of his nonsense. He probably stole this bottle from some vendor." She waved the lamp in his face, causing Girl to growl in the background. "Go on with you now, get away from here, or I'll put the servants on you. You've wasted enough of our time."

"Yes," Arron added, "take your coin and count yourself lucky. It's a sight more than you're worth."

At a nod from him, a servant reached for the gate and began pulling it to. Before it could close, Magda surprised herself by speaking out on Boy's behalf.

"He's a gifted water diviner, did you know that?" she half shouted. "He found the water in that bottle himself. He …!"

The gate swung into its frame with a crash. And Boy, like a wild creature in pain, let out a long howling cry.

"Hush!" Magda said with concern, pressing her fingers to his mouth. "Enough."

Yet despite her advice, she could not resist a parting shot of her own. "I could tell you what he's really worth!" she yelled through the gate. "And it's a lot more than a copper coin. More than all the gold you've got in that purse of yours! Except you're too blind to see it!"

She was still muttering angrily as they trooped off through the dark, heading back to the city. Boy, for his part, said nothing. When they reached the first of the cramped lanes, he stopped in a poorly lit doorway and peered at something in his hand.

"What is it?" Magda asked.

He showed her the copper coin, and then did something that caught her unawares. Taking off one of his necklaces, he fashioned a section of string into a series of loops that he tightened around the coin. Once it was securely held, he slipped the necklace back on.

She did not think to ask him what he was doing, the answer already plain to see. Not just in the changed meaning of the necklace, but in his face—a look of deadly intent there, that made her wince and glance away.

"One … charm," he explained, in case she had failed to understand. "Best … one."

"No, not the best!" she burst out. "The worst! You can't live by that! If you do, you'll be no better than those people in the House of Rain."

"Yes … same," he agreed evenly. "Same … like them … always."

And now there was something about his tone that struck at her dearest hopes for him. So that suddenly she did not dare look into his eyes, for fear of what she might see.

"Is this how you mean to live?" she asked in a frightened voice. "For coin? For gold? For what people will pay you? Is this what you understand by being special? Is it?"

She could have borne it had he answered her with another of his howling cries. What he did instead she found far harder to bear. Pressing the coin into the skin of his chest, he held it there for some moments.

"No!" she moaned, hiding her eyes.

He released it at last and let it swing free. By then, clearly imprinted on his flesh, was the coin's round outline.

PART IV

the man

16

He sought out his new-found companions the next morning. They were busy at the well, making it deeper, wider, and they thought at first he had come to claim a larger share. He quickly assured them that his original word held: the well was theirs, to do with as they pleased. The other wells were all that concerned him now.

Kris looked up sharply from her work. "*Other* wells? You mean you can find more like this?"

Boy opened his arms wide, as if to embrace the whole valley. "Many ... many ... many ..."

Petro also abandoned his work, his dark eyes gleaming. Even Jude, the most relaxed of the three, showed interest.

They sat in the sand after that and bargained. It was there that Magda and Girl found them some hours later, though by then the hard bargaining was over. They had agreed that Boy would find the wells and claim half the money earned. For the other half, Kris and her friends would do all the digging, as well as cart the water to market and supervise its sale. Petro, of course, was given the task of hiring water bags and camels; Jude would keep the wells in working order and see to the loading; Kris would trade the water for gold in the central market.

To close the deal, they spat on their palms and shook hands—all, that is, except for Magda.

"There's nothing for me to do," she said forlornly.

Boy patted her shoulder, as if she were the child and he the adult.

"You ... go market ... too," he told her. "You ... buy food ... make fire ... you ... you ... mother."

She bridled at the word *mother*. "No, I'm unfit," she said. "A servant is all I've ever been."

Boy, in turn, refused to see her as a servant. "No ... friend," he insisted. "Good friend ... always."

And that was how their new life began. Within days, Boy had located underground streams all across the delta, and as fast as the others dug down to them, he found more. Because they had no money as yet, and could not afford camels, they carried the first load of water to market on their shoulders. The traders laughed when they staggered into the central square, laden with cheap earthenware bottles, but the laughter soon turned to astonishment when the water was tasted. Minutes later, those same traders were vying with each other to buy it.

The gold they earned was spent on leather water bags and the hiring of camels—which earned them more gold to spend on their other wells. Until after a month, they were carting more good water to market than any other vendor.

Meanwhile, they continued to sleep under the stars, like hundreds of other homeless people, and to cook their food on an open fire fueled by dry camel dung.

One evening, sitting around the fire after a meal, Kris voiced aloud her discontent.

"Why are we still living like beggars?" she complained. "We're earning more than we've ever dreamed of. I say we spend a little gold on ourselves."

"No, more camels are what we need," Petro argued. "Our wells are producing ten times as much as we can load."

Jude, as usual, had mixed feelings. Although he yearned

for a soft bed and an easier life, he also relished the thought of further riches. So it was left to Boy to decide the issue.

Fingering the copper coin on his necklace, he gazed into the flaming coals, as though he could see the future. "One … day," he began slowly, "all wells … only for us … all water … only for us."

Magda shifted uneasily in the shadows. "The Great Father owns the water beneath the land," she reminded him.

"So they say," Jude half agreed with a yawn.

"No … for us … now," Boy said, ramming one fist into another. "We take … we keep."

"Yeah, but what about the gold we're earning?" Kris pressed him.

He fixed her with the same look of deadly intent that Magda had observed weeks earlier, on the night of his great disappointment. "We … no spend … for us yet. We wait. We spend … first for wells … first for camels … first for water bags. We … we own … much … much …"

"How much?" Magda broke in.

He turned and stared past her as if she hardly existed, his eyes probing the dark in the direction of the ocean.

"We … own more … than … than House of Rain," he finished softly.

The discussion ended there, and was not taken up again for many months. By then, their wells dominated the delta; their strings of camels (owned now, not hired) outnumbered all others; they occupied the most honored place at the central market.

And still Boy searched out fresh sources of water, like someone driven by an unquenchable thirst. Though, in fact, they already produced more water than they could sell; and they earned more gold than they could spend—more even than they could safely hide from the curious eyes of beggars. Weeks before, they had been forced to load their excess gold onto camels and cart it off to the bankers who occupied the great money-changing houses flanking the marketplace. Glittering bags of it now sat in underground vaults that were kept locked and guarded day and night.

It was after yet another trip to these vaults that Kris renewed her complaint about the way they were living.

"Look at us," she said, indicating their makeshift camp-site on the open riverbed. "A year's gone by since we dug our first well, and here we are, still camped on the sand. Anyone would think we're penniless, whereas we're probably richer than anyone in Delta."

Boy, whose speech had begun to improve in recent months, looked at her with interest.

"We ... rich enough for ... for buying ... land maybe?"

"Yes, land, houses, anything we want."

Petro put aside the leather harness he was fixing. "Our camels alone are worth more than any single house."

"Yeah, and that includes the big houses facing the river," Jude added carelessly.

To which Boy said nothing at all, his eyes again fixed broodingly on the burning heart of the fire.

The following morning, he did not rouse Girl and go out, as usual, in search of new wells. Instead, he left Girl with Magda and went to the money-changing houses in the city. From there, in company with the chief banker, he made his way to the great mansions that stood close to where the delta met the sea. All day he bargained, and by nightfall he owned not only the mansion on the farthermost point of land, but also the smaller dwelling beside it—the one people called the House of Rain.

A week later, he stood beside the seawall, bare-headed in

the fierce sunlight, and waited as furniture and goods were carried from the House of Rain and loaded onto donkey-drawn carts. Arron and Elvina emerged last of all. To his surprise, they no longer looked resplendent in their scarlet robes. To his more adult gaze, the robes themselves appeared faded and worn. As for the two so-called rainmakers—how wizened and mean they seemed; how greedy the eyes they turned in his direction.

Seeing him standing by the wall, they walked over, words of greeting on their lips; but he turned his back and faced out to sea, refusing to acknowledge them.

"This is unkind," he heard Elvina say. "It's no way to treat people you've had dealings with."

He turned then and showed her the copper coin he wore, willing her to remember. She stared blankly back at him, however, remembering nothing, and he let them go without a word, the taste of ashes on his tongue.

That night, he put a torch to the House of Rain and watched it burn. Magda watched with him, lamenting the way the flames licked up around the windows and doors.

"Aah, the waste of it," she sighed. "Such a fine house."

"Cursed … house," he muttered, and would have walked away, had she not caught at his sleeve.

"Why cursed? You longed to live there once. To become a rainmaker."

"No one … make rain," he said coldly. "The skies … they empty … like … like house."

"They won't always be empty," she reasoned. "The Great Father will weep for us if we're patient. He always does in the end."

"No weep … for me," he answered in the same cold voice. "No weep … for House of Rain. See …" He pointed to the leaping flames and glowing roof beams. "House …

is finished … rain too … finished. Now … we have … wells only."

"And gold, always gold," she added in a sad whisper.

In the bleak light of early morning, he walked alone among the smoking ruins. For a single moment, as he gazed from the blackened courtyard, out toward the seawall, he recalled a young boy who had stood there once. How long ago? Hardly more than a year, though it felt ten times longer. In his imagination, their eyes met—his and the boy's—and he felt tears prickling at the backs of his eyes.

Where had that young boy gone?

With a quick turn of the head, he dismissed the boy from thought. Clear-eyed once again, he surveyed the smoke-stained walls and charred roof beams, already picturing to himself what would replace them.

A few days later, the ruins had been cleared away and new structures began to rise in their place. Some were stables for his camels. Others were storage sheds for his leather water bags and earthenware bottles. Others again were intended as lowly accommodation for his many servants.

He watched this rebuilding from the neighboring mansion, where he now lived; watched it with the same cold eyes that had witnessed the fire—his fingers all the while stroking the copper coin at his throat. There was no wall surrounding these buildings, no entrance gate. Yet despite this difference, they often reminded him of the original house, and he would feel suddenly lost, his throat dryer than an abandoned well.

"Magda!" he would call at such times. "Magda! Come see."

She always answered his summons, though she hated to look down upon the stables. Plain and windowless, fit only for beasts, she saw in them the end of all his dreams.

"I have so much to do," she would say impatiently. "So many servants to keep busy." And she would hurry away and leave him to this new kind of vigil.

By day, he still went out in search of wells. Sometimes he took Girl along, but mostly he ignored her whining pleas and left her behind. For unlike Girl, he rarely made mistakes. The mere smell of the sand warned him of stagnant water; the taste of it indicated how far underground a stream lay; and when he marked a spot for digging, he knew within a hand's breadth how deep Jude would have to delve.

As his wealth and fame grew, he took to wearing fine clothes—long flowing robes of white. He also took to riding a pure white camel, a huge beast that clattered along, scattering beggars from its path. If he was in a generous mood, he threw coins to the beggars, and nodded in recognition when they called him rainmaker or shaman.

Why bother to argue, when it was plain to everyone that he was the only genuine shaman in Delta? For who else could find water as he did? Who else could conjure gold from dry sand? True, he could not make the rain fall. But he was now of the opinion that such power lay beyond the grasp of any man, himself included. It was enough to be revered as a shaman—a wise finder of water—and for beggars and citizens alike to touch their foreheads to the sand as he rode by.

In keeping with his new and lofty status, he abandoned the charms he had worn since childhood. The skull, he considered unsightly; the feather too frayed, its silken sheen faded by the years; the claw too old and cracked; and the stone ... well, it was just an ordinary river stone, not something to be worn with pride. In their place, he wore a single necklace of golden links, with the copper coin attached.

He liked showing off the coin, and explaining how it

was the first money he had earned with his shaman skills. Many people pretended to be interested, but few were. It was his gold alone that interested them. What, after all, was a copper coin compared to such huge wealth? He saw the emptiness in their faces, and their false smiles—he was not a fool—but these things didn't really bother him. He had friends enough in Kris, Jude, and Petro ... and, oh yes, in Magda and Girl too. Except that these last were not so much friends as old acquaintances, beings he knew as intimately as he thought he knew himself.

At the end of every week, they met together in the mansion by the sea and drank fine wines that came in ships from foreign lands. By midnight, they were drunk, laughing together as Petro danced a crazed dance that always ended in tears of sorrow and regret.

"Why me ...?" Petro would moan, the sparkle gone from his eyes. "What did I do to deserve this hump? These dwarf legs?"

Together, they showered him with gold, to ease his pain; but he always scooped the coins aside and reached instead for his wine cup.

So did Jude, who had married a local beauty and found only misery. Now, his beard much longer, and tied in a series of sad knots, he slurped at his wine as readily as Petro.

Kris was not much better off. The man she loved had dedicated himself to ancient learning, and disapproved of her wealth. So she also drank to forget.

Over them all presided Boy, whose powers of speech were now almost perfect. In the small hours of the night, when the others had fallen into drunken sleep, he would ramble on about his noble birth; stagger out onto the marble-flagged porch and tell the stars how he was sired by the Great Father; crawl as far as the lapping ocean and whisper to the waves how he had issued from the womb of the Earth Mother herself.

In time, he came to believe these fictions. His skills as a shaman seemed to render them true. For those skills had to come from somewhere; they had to have a beginning, a *noble* beginning. They could not have just happened to an ordinary boy … a fatherless waif … a foundling. No, that was unthinkable. High-born parents and a fabulous birth were the only way to explain all that he had become.

In this daze of false grandeur, another year of his life slipped by … and another. More often drunk than sober, he began to neglect his wells. He searched out no new ones, and left the upkeep of the others to Jude. That was the agreement after all: for Jude to service the wells; Petro to transport the water; and Kris to attend the market. Weren't they paid enough for their paltry labor? A full half share no less! Far more than they were worth. So why should he, the greatest man in Delta, stoop to rambling around the riverbed sniffing out wells like a common hound? Or devote precious time to helping his friends, come to that?

Increasingly, he remained alone within his mansion, staring sullenly out to sea. Magda brought him his meals as always, but otherwise he hardly registered her presence. It was the same with Girl. All but forgotten, she slept away her days in the courtyard, or hunted along the seashore where she dug up empty shells and snapped at the few half-starved gulls that soared above the waves.

Soon, even the gulls disappeared, as the drought bit deeper. Not a drop of rain had fallen in years. No rumble of thunder sounded across the plain; no flicker of lightning showed in the distant sky. People claimed it was dryer than ever before; that the land was cursed. Many began to leave the city in order to seek a life elsewhere. The ships that brought wines and other goods now carried these people away to far-off lands—where, it was said, clouds still gathered in the evening sky and rain fell gently to earth.

As the city emptied, the need for water decreased, and the flow of gold at the market fell to a trickle. But Boy didn't care about that either. He was wealthy enough to last ten lifetimes. Why, most of the gold in the city vaults belonged either to him or to his companions.

Those companions still visited his mansion, but less often; and when they did meet together, they seemed to have lost the knack of laughter. Petro no longer danced on the table, nor threw himself down in despair, lamenting his fate. He spent the evenings sullen and drunk, gazing out to sea with dull eyes. Jude grumbled endlessly about how hard he worked at the wells, and how one after the other they were drying up, despite all his efforts. Kris, originally the most cheerful of them all, took to weeping quietly to herself, or singing wistful songs about lost love. As for Boy, these days he paid little attention either to his companions or to their troubles. What did their foolish lives matter to someone of his exalted position? More and more, his gaze turned inward, toward that vacant space within himself which, puzzlingly, no amount of fame or gold could fill.

At last, sadly neglected by him, his one-time friends ceased to come altogether. He did not notice their absence at first. As the months dragged by, however, and his isolation deepened, he began to miss them. He recalled their shared evenings with a desperate kind of longing; and he ached for the clatter of the bell at the gate, announcing their arrival.

One morning, when he could bear the loneliness no longer, he asked Magda: "What has happened to Kris and the others?"

Magda shrugged vaguely, refusing to meet his eye. "Gone, I expect," she muttered. "Like everyone else."

"Everyone?"

"Those who had any sense left long ago," she said darkly.

He gave a pained laugh. "Does that mean the rest of us are fools for staying?"

"Some of us are," she said, and there was something about her tone that made him look keenly at her.

"Magda!" he said in surprise. "Your hair! It's turned white!"

"So I've been told."

"But how …? When …? I mean, I never noticed before."

She looked directly at him. "There are many things you haven't noticed," she said, and returned to the kitchen.

That conversation, although brief, unsettled him further. His meal over, he felt restless, unable to sit and look at the sea. Driven by he knew not what, he left the house for the first time in weeks and wandered over to the stables.

"Petro," he shouted as he approached the closed doors. "Petro, prepare my white camel. I mean to ride out."

There was no answer, and when he heaved the doors open, he found the stables empty, the stalls heaped with stale straw.

It was much the same when he walked back along the delta later in the day. The jugglers, the acrobats, the well diggers, the strings of camels … all had vanished. The riverbed was now hardly more than a wasteland. A few wells still functioned, but not many, and none was his. Of Jude there was no sign at all.

When he walked into the city, he could not find Kris either. He searched the deserted marketplace in vain; and after that the empty halls where once the money changers had sat. Of all the familiar faces, only one remained: the chief banker, an old man too set in his ways to leave.

"Kris …?" the banker said thoughtfully, plucking at his beard. "Yes, I do recall her. A pretty girl, but sad. She did well to take ship away from here."

"She left? Without telling me?"

"These are trying times," the old man sighed. "They test the best of friendships. But never fear, good sir, she took none of your gold with her."

"I didn't think she would," Boy said sadly.

"Oh no, I wouldn't have allowed it," the old man rambled on. "Your precious coin sits safely in my vault, like always. Some things, I'm glad to say, are changeless, and gold is one. Would you not agree, good sir?"

"Yes, gold remains," Boy muttered in reply, and left the banker to his keys and accounts.

Walking off through the lonely streets, he thought sorrowfully of his three lost companions, and of how they had departed without so much as a farewell. Had they cared so little for him? Was gold, perhaps, the only cement binding their friendship together? And when they had wealth enough, had the binding somehow come undone? But then, why leave without a word? It didn't make sense. He was the same person he had always been. Or so he told himself—so he needed to believe. Why flee from him then?

In his bewilderment, he felt beneath his tunic for the copper coin that lay close to his heart. As always, he found a certain comfort in its cool touch. Fingering the worn metal, he thought bitterly: let them go, I'm better off without them.

Yet hours later, back at the mansion, his sense of emptiness returned. Pacing the upper terrace in the cool of the evening, he felt a wordless misery rise up inside him. A choking sob caught in his throat. And at that precise instant, he heard something. A faint rumbling. A low growl from the direction of the mountains.

He felt a small lift of hope. Almost of joy.

Could it be ...? Could it possibly be ...?

He stood stock-still and listened hard, straining for the least sound ... but the night had fallen silent, the stillness broken only by the lapping of ocean waves.

No, impossible! he decided wretchedly, and resumed his pacing.

17

Three nights later, Boy heard more distant rumbling from the mountains.

Only minutes earlier, he had called to Magda and received no answer. The kitchen he had found empty. Her bedroom was equally deserted, her few belongings missing. Close to panic, he had gone in search of Girl, but she too had disappeared, the courtyard gate swinging in the wind.

It was as he stood there staring at the open gate, stifling his grief, that the thunder sounded: faint, but quite distinct.

A further wave of grief threatened to overwhelm him, and with it came more mutterings from the far-off peaks. In the silence that followed, the walls of the house seemed to close in. This mansion he had occupied with such pride suddenly felt more like a prison than a home; a lonely cell that he shared with no one.

It came to him then, the most unwelcome of truths: that he was not in fact a great shaman, and never had been. He was a finder of wells, nothing else, and he had sold his modest gift for gold.

Crossing the courtyard at a run, he emerged onto the strand above the sea. In the faint starlight, he could see that nobody walked the shoreline; no playful animal splashed among the shallows.

"M-a-g-d-a! G-i-r-l!" he called in despair, his voice rising to a woeful howl.

When nobody answered, he reverted to the almost forgotten ways of his boyhood. Raising his head, he sniffed the offshore breeze; searched it for a familiar scent ... and caught a tang of something! Yes, they had come this way! They had turned inland, set their faces toward the dry, gusting wind that blew straight from the mountains.

Like a hound on a trail, he followed them. The lingering scent of their passage wound back along the road to the city, and from there out onto the delta. He dogged their footsteps through the scattering of now-ruined wells; past the tumbledown remains of fringe-dweller camps; and along to a section of riverbank where a few hardy palms struggled to survive.

There, beneath rustling palm fronds, he came upon a white-haired figure kneeling in the sand. She did not turn at his approach.

"I'm not coming back," she told him.

"Why not?"

"Because it isn't my home."

"It's mine and Girl's. Isn't that enough for you?"

"It's not Girl's either," Magda said, and pointed to where the riverbank was hollowed out to form a shallow cave.

He moved closer and peered in. Something stirred in there. Girl? She was lying full-stretch on the sand, her head raised slightly as she stared back at him.

Puzzled, he glanced across at Magda. "Is she sick?"

"No, not sick. Unless, of course, you think motherhood is an illness."

"*Motherhood?*"

"She's been true to her line and given birth late in life, like her mother before her."

"Given *birth*?" He was unsure whether to feel joy for Girl's sake, or sadness that she should have abandoned him at such a time. "I don't understand," he confessed with a shake of the head. "She could have whelped in the courtyard … in the house itself … anywhere she wanted. She must know I would have …"

"This is what she wanted," Magda interrupted. "I followed her here. This was the place she chose."

"But why here? It's dangerous. I heard thunder earlier. The river could flood and wash her away."

Magda allowed herself a soft chuckle. "Girl may be a dog, but she isn't a fool. She knows that rain has left the land. For the present, this riverbank is as safe a haven as any. In any case, I've been here all along."

"Why you?" he said, stung afresh by feelings of rejection. "Why not me?"

"Because … because females prefer their own kind around them at such times. We understand what needs to be done, and what … what help to give."

Something about Magda's tone alerted him.

"Help?" he queried sharply. "Did she have trouble birthing?"

A sliver of moon had risen to the right of Magda's shoulder. By its faint light, he saw her hang her head and press her hand to her throat in sorrow.

"Three of them lie buried here," she said, smoothing the sand between her knees.

"There were more?"

"A fourth, but a weakling. A tiny female. When I last looked, she was hanging to life by a thread."

Boy crawled closer to Girl's den and reached inside. As his groping hand touched her flank, she growled and turned. Her teeth closed around his wrist, hard enough to hold him but not puncture the skin.

"It's me," he murmured. "A friend."

Slowly she slackened her grip; licked at where the tooth

marks still dented the flesh. And he felt between her legs for the pup.

It squirmed and nuzzled at his fingers when he picked it up, hunting for the teat. He held it against his pure white robe, and its searching mouth caught at a fold in the cloth and sucked feebly.

"Will it live?" he asked Magda in a whisper, as if she alone understood the ways of the natural world.

Magda let out a weary sigh. "Who can say? This is how Girl began her life, so perhaps ... But no, it's foolish to hope. We can only wait and see."

Foolish or not, Boy clung desperately to hope as the night advanced. He had given the pup back to Girl; placed it next to a teat; smeared milk on its snout. There was nothing more to be done after that, and like Magda—though with none of her resignation—he set himself to wait.

Dawn found them both sprawled upon the sand, fast asleep. Bleary-eyed, Boy rose and checked on Girl, who whimpered a welcome. The pup slept on, its blunt snout stained with faint streaks of white. Was that the remains of the milk he had smeared there? Or the result of the pup's feeding? He had no way of telling.

Once again, all he could do was wait. Or was it?

Reaching over, he shook Magda awake. "A name!" he said urgently. "We need a name!"

"What ...?" She gazed sleepily up at him.

"When Girl was born—do you remember?—you said we should give her a name. To hold her here in the world of the living. Well, we must do the same now."

Magda blinked the sleep from her eyes. "Girl is the daughter of your sister. The granddaughter of your mother. It's for you to give her pup a name, not me."

He thought of all he had gained and lost in recent years, hunting through memory for a single word that would sum up the best of his life. It came to him without effort, though he could not have explained why it felt so right.

"Faith," he said. "I'll call her Faith."

He was even more mystified by the way Magda suddenly gave way to tears. "Yes," she agreed, "it's the perfect name. That will keep her here."

Despite Magda's confidence, the pup did not rally. Throughout the day and the following night, it lingered on, taking a little milk, but not enough to grow in strength. Girl, on the other hand, recovered quickly. She seemed puzzled more than saddened by her pup's weakness. She would lick at it occasionally, and even take it in her mouth and place it by the teat; and when it turned away its small blind face, she would whimper her bewilderment.

Boy filled the dragging hours by making himself useful. He located an underground stream, close to the bank, and dug a shallow well. Later, he walked into the city to buy bread and dates, and some dried meat for Girl. There were only a few stalls at the food market, so prices were high. Finding that he had little money in his purse, he hesitated for a moment and finally bartered his gold necklace.

The stall-holder pulled the copper coin free of its gold links and offered it back to him.

"I won't be needing this," he said with a frown.

Boy almost accepted it; then something prompted him to close the man's fingers around the coin.

"No, it was a keepsake once," he said, "but now I'm done with it."

Again, he did not fully understand his own motives. Yet like the pup's name—Faith—this giving up of his keepsake also seemed right.

He felt naked without a necklace, however, and rather than return to the riverbank immediately, he walked on toward his mansion. It took some little while to find the old necklaces, which he had discarded so carelessly. He discovered them at last in a sandalwood trunk that had not been opened in years. The skull had browned with the passage of time; the claw and feather looked more battered than ever; the river stone was exactly that—an ordinary pebble. With a rueful smile, he slipped the cords over his neck, but now the whiteness of his robe made the charms appear more humble still. He almost cast them aside again ... decided against it, and changed his robe instead: for a simple tunic of the kind worn by servants.

On the point of leaving the house, he remembered his empty purse and went to another trunk, where he kept a store of money. A fistful of coins was enough to buy food for the next week or more; but having filled his purse, his hand dipped back into the trunk almost of its own accord.

Have I grown greedy with age? he wondered—though in fact it wasn't greed that drove him, not at that moment. It was thoughts of Magda: confused thoughts that he could not untangle. On impulse, he selected a small leather bag filled with gold coin, which he slipped beneath his tunic.

He left the house in the failing light, pulling the gate to with a clang. Halfway along the road to the city, he looked back just once. It was easy to pick out his mansion, which loomed like a pale shadow against the backdrop of the ocean. How huge and formless it looked. How dark and deserted now that lamps no longer burned at the windows. Such a house needed warmth and light, children and laughter to fill its rooms. He had not been fit to live there, he could see that now. With a slight shrug of the shoulders—as if to say, What does it matter if I never return?—he hurried on his way.

The moon had barely risen when he reached Girl's den in the riverbank. She leaped toward him when she smelled the dried meat he brought, and he tossed her several pieces. While she was bolting them down, he looked toward Magda, sitting hunched and still before a small fire of palm fronds.

She gave a nod of quiet contentment when she saw the necklaces he wore.

"Is this the Boy I used to know?" she mused aloud.

"No, I think he's gone forever," he answered truthfully.

She shook her head—whether in doubt or sorrow he could not tell—and directed his gaze to the shadowy den.

"Faith lingers on," she murmured. "Only time will decide."

Side by side in the firelight, they prepared themselves for another long night of waiting. Waking and dozing in turns, they saw out the first few hours. But soon after midnight, Boy came to with a sudden jolt and knew instantly that things had changed.

"Faith!" he called softly through the dark. "Faith!" And heard a mewing answer from the den.

He scrambled toward the opening and discovered with relief that the pup was feeding. He could feel its mouth sucking rhythmically, its paws blindly kneading the teat to increase the milk's flow.

He was hardly conscious of Magda shuffling up beside him; of her hands reaching past his, feeling for the pup.

"Saved!" he heard a voice breathe close to his ear.

He slept soundly after that, and woke shortly before dawn. Going once more to the den, he lifted the pup, who nuzzled his chest and nestled close to the skull he wore. Holding it near, he climbed the bank and sat beneath the palm trees, where he waited for first light.

As usual, it seemed never to come. The final hour of dark

stretched on and on. The moon had set, the stars shone hard and bright, and he gazed up into the blackness, willing it to reveal the future. But all he glimpsed there were images from his past, some more imagined than real. Himself as a baby, whirled along by the flood, his infant fist bunched around a river pebble. A flurry of golden wings as the high peaks spoke to him in the language of beak and talon. The bright tongue of flame that had reached from the fire and run its burning tip across his back. And not least, the roaring challenge of a great bear, followed by his own baby laughter as he staggered forward to greet it.

What did any of these images mean? What did they tell him about the here and now, or the days to come? He had no idea. Better to block them out; to close his eyes against the night and forget.

He hadn't meant to sleep. When he next looked up the dawn had arrived. He was lying sprawled beneath a palm tree, the pup still cradled in his arms, and Magda was gazing down at him.

"It's time to go home," she announced.

He sat up and dusted the sand from his hair.

"Time for *you* to go home, maybe," he said. "Me, I belong nowhere."

She took the pup from him, kissed its unopened eyes, and held it out to the newly risen sun as a kind of offering.

"He doesn't think there's a place to call his own," she told the sun-bright puppy face, "but he's wrong. Because the village will find room for him, like before. It will find room for you too," she added, handing the puppy back. "Here, have Faith," she said, and laughed at her own small joke.

"The village isn't for me," he said seriously. "I'm no farmer. I'm not even a hunter any longer. I'd have nothing to do there."

"You could make the rain fall again," she suggested slyly.

It was his turn to laugh. "Think what you please, Magda, but I'm telling you now, I'm no shaman either. Nor ever will be. Although I can find water, I can't coax it from the skies. Nobody can do that."

"Nobody?"

"A very great shaman perhaps," he conceded. "Not me."

She pondered his reply for some moments. "So if you're not a great shaman, what are you?"

"I'm not sure," he confessed. "To the people of Delta, I'm a water diviner. To the people of the village—and to Girl too—I suppose I'm still a dogboy."

"Yes, but what are you really?" she pressed him.

Unable to answer, he looked into her eyes and saw a reflection of himself that he barely recognized.

"Tell me," he pleaded.

"To me," she said slowly, "you are many things. You are the son I wished for; a gift from the Great Father; and a child of the wild river. But above all else ..." She paused, as though weighing each word with care, "... above all else, you are the rainchild."

He could not explain why her closing words moved him so. He stared straight past her, into the living soul of the risen sun, and felt the brightness force tears from his eyes. For the third time in the past week, he heard the murmur of thunder, a long rumbling call from the high peaks.

When he turned in their direction, he could see no clouds—only the washed-out blue of early morning sky. But it made no difference, for he knew in his heart that he was being summoned.

"You're right," he told Magda, climbing slowly to his feet, young Faith held securely in his arms. "It's time to go home."

18

Boy made no attempt to sell his mansion. Who would have bought it in those worsening times of drought, the city emptying by the day? Nor did he visit the old banker who held the keys to his stored wealth. He preferred to leave the city as he had first approached it: not splendidly dressed and mounted on a milk-white camel; but on foot, and with few possessions apart from the simple clothes he wore.

As it happened, Magda was more burdened than he, for she had wrapped her extra clothes and trinkets in a shawl, which she carried on her back. Noticing how stiffly she walked—the years of hard work having taken their toll—he offered to carry the bundle for her, but she wouldn't hear of it.

"No, it's for you to look after Faith," she said. "Whether she survives this journey is in your hands."

To make the pup more comfortable, he wove for her a soft basket, made from palm fronds, which he hung from one shoulder. Then together—Boy, Girl, Magda, and Faith—they set off upriver.

He had thought to return to the land of his childhood as a nobody; as just one more refugee bent on escaping the drought-ridden city. He was even prepared for a show of hostility from those they met. In recent months there had been many refugees, after all, every one of them seeking water, food, shelter. So it was understandable if the upriver folk felt invaded; if they feared that their precious resources were at risk.

What he was *not* prepared for—what took him entirely by surprise—was the reception he was given by the first of the river guardians they came upon. Led by a tall, imposing man in long black robes, the entire group dropped to their knees and touched their foreheads to the sand.

Clearly, his fame had spread.

"Welcome, lord," the man said reverently.

"I'm no lord," Boy replied. "I'm a poor traveler, just one among many."

"Not so, lord," the man contradicted him gently. "You are the giver of water, the bringer of life."

A sudden thought occurred to Boy. "How do you know who I am?"

"I was a youth, like you, when you passed this way in years gone by. I recognized you, lord. We have keen eyes on this part of the river, and I spotted you from afar."

"Am I so little changed?" Boy asked, amazed, for secretly he felt that the thread binding him to his youthful self had been severed by his time in Delta.

"We all change, lord," the man answered, fingering his own luxuriant beard. "But who we really are … that remains. The being within shines through. And you, lord, have always been a giver of water. This I know."

Boy squatted on the sand beside him. "I see that the time has come to strike a bargain."

"A bargain, lord?"

"Yes, our safe passage in exchange for wells."

There were murmurs of dismay from the rest of the group, and their leader shook his head firmly.

"No, lord, there is no question of a bargain between us. Safe passage is the right of any shaman. You may pass safely through our land whenever it pleases you. All we seek here is a gift: the blessing of water from your hand. You are free to withhold or bestow it as you wish."

Humbled, Boy covered his face with both hands. "It seems I brought a curse, not a blessing, to the city of Delta," he confessed.

"Not you, lord," the man said confidently. "The Great Father punishes us all from time to time, whether we will it or not. It is the sole task of the true shaman to *win back* His favor."

"But I sold my talent for gold," Boy muttered to his closed hands.

"Which of us is without fault, lord?" came the reply. "Still you brought water to the city. Children and their families lived because of you. Was this not a blessing?"

When he made no answer, the man reached out and placed a comforting hand on his shoulder, as though offering him forgiveness.

Boy removed his hands from his face. Rising to his feet, he walked out across the riverbed for some hundreds of paces, the others trailing behind. At last he stopped and pointed to a spot in the sand.

"Dig your first well here," he told them. "It is not a gift. If I have the right of safe passage, then this too is yours by right. We stand equal."

"Never, lord!" a woman answered fervently.

He did not answer her immediately. He dropped to his knees instead, and scooped at the sand until fresh water gushed up from below. Filling both cupped hands, he went to the woman and offered her the water, as one equal to another.

"Drink," he said, and raised it to her lips.

That proved to be the first of many wells he picked out

for them. On each occasion, he insisted that this well, like the one before, was theirs by right. For weren't they the river guardians? They accepted his view eventually; though no argument of his could prevent them calling him lord. According to their leader, the Great Father was merciful at heart, because for every drought He inflicted on the land, He also granted the people a great shaman, to counter it.

"You are he, lord," he told Boy.

Those were his closing words at parting, near the upriver boundary, where he and Boy touched foreheads and smiled the smiles of abiding friendship.

The guardians they met after that treated him with the same unfailing respect. "The giver of water" was their name for him, and in a land where water was valued above gold, no title conveyed more honor. By day, people begged to carry him over the rougher, stonier ground, and were deeply disappointed when he insisted on walking. By night, they made him soft beds from the leafy branches of hardy desert plants, and looked on in bewilderment as he offered the beds to Girl and Faith.

"Is a dog now greater than a man?" an old woman quizzed him.

"I was reared by a dog," he said, and he showed her the skull he wore.

She examined it curiously, before raising her eyes to his. "Is this then your secret?"

"My secret …?"

"The reason why you are who you are. Is it because you have seen the world through the eyes of a dog? Is this why the land speaks back to you?"

No one had ever put that idea to him before, and he pondered it in the days that followed. Walking between wells, or lying sleepless at night, gazing at the stars, he wondered whether his dog nature was in truth his only talent. Before he could come to any conclusions, another old woman, farther upriver, merely added to the puzzle.

Pointing to his other charms—the claw, the feather, and the stone—she asked him what magic they contained.

"The magic of memory, that's all," he answered.

She, too, screwed up her eyes and examined them more closely. "So they have no power of their own?" she demanded. "This power over water, it all comes from you?"

He had no ready answer to that either, and he withdrew more deeply into himself as he pondered these mysteries.

Wrestling with them night after night, he was unconscious at first of Magda looking at him askance. Then one day, as he stood apart from the well diggers, sunk in thought, she challenged him.

"This is how you lost your way before," she said, "years ago, when we were journeying downriver. I watched it happen: how you loved the praise people showered on you; how you were changed by it."

He remembered those days, and understood that what she said was partly true. Pride, like an evil bloom, had flowered in him then. But not any longer. How could he take pride in failure? How could he glory in this present praise, lavished on him by the river guardians, when he knew himself to be a sham?

Pointing to the well diggers, he said to Magda: "Of these many people here, I fear I am the least. That's all that fills my mind, not pride."

"Why the least?" she asked.

He placed a hand on his charms. "Without these, and without my dog upbringing, what am I?"

"No, you are special," she said, unwilling to condemn him completely.

"Only because of these charms," he answered her, "and because of these people who believe in me. Theirs is the power, not mine. In truth, I'm just a *finder* of water, not the giver they take me for."

"Finders of water can also be blessed," she assured him, "but not if they practice their art with a proud spirit. The vain are a curse to all, themselves included. Phylo taught me that when I stood as a small child at his knee."

"At *Phylo's* knee?" Boy realized all at once that he knew little about Magda's girlhood. "You speak of Phylo as if he were your parent."

"In a way he was. I was a foundling like you, left at his door in the depths of the night. He and Nessa took me in. As a child, I earned my keep by doing chores, and became their servant in later years."

"So you were raised as a servant," he said pensively, adding as an afterthought: "Therefore you became one."

"And …?" she prompted him.

He shrugged. "I was raised as a dog, so what does that make me?"

"You were also cared for by the river," she countered. "It kept you safe. It delivered you to our door."

"Dogboy … riverboy, what's the difference? As I said before, I'm still the least of these people here and don't deserve their praise."

Magda gave a relieved smile. "Spoken like a true rain-child," she said, and walked away.

After several weeks of slow travel, they arrived at the boundary Boy had been dreading: that section of riverbed guarded by the family who had imprisoned and tortured him. Bidding farewell to the previous guardians, they trudged on through the sand, meeting no one for some time. At a bend in the river, however, they were hailed by a figure on the far bank.

Boy's first instinct was to retreat. Before he could take a backward step, a loosed arrow thudded into the sand at his feet. Casting a nervous glance skyward, he reached down and plucked the arrow free. Attached to its shaft was a type of leather cocoon; and inside the cocoon, three small nuggets of alluvial gold, no doubt sifted from the river.

"It looks like payment of some kind," Magda said.

"Yes, but for what?"

Warily, using his own body as a shield for the others, he approached the riverbank. The figure who had hailed him moments before had disappeared, but when he climbed higher, he was met by the whole family, kneeling humbly among the saltbush and stones and shriveled cactus.

"Why did you give me these?" he asked, tossing the nuggets down into the dust.

The man, older and more grizzled, looked up at him with the same ugly eyes. "They are the price of forgiveness, lord."

"Forgiveness has no price," he answered. "Not a price that can be measured in gold. It is something that can only be earned."

One of the daughters, now a fine young woman, shuffled nearer. "Instruct us, lord. Tell us how to undo past evils."

Again it was a question he was not sure how to answer. He had to think for a while, before saying: "The cage you kept me in, do you still have it?"

"Yes, lord. Sometimes, when we trap gazelles, we put them in the cage until we need the meat."

"Then take me to it," he said.

In an uneasy silence—broken only by Faith, who yipped happily as she trotted among them—they trudged as far as the track that led up to the house. There, at the top of the hill and still tied to a roof-pole, was the cage. Its plaited reed bars had become frayed from long use, but it was still sturdy and strong.

At the sight of it, Girl whimpered and crowded in close against Boy's legs.

"Shush now," he murmured, his voice low and for her ears alone. "We're about the business of forgiveness here, not suffering."

She quieted down, reassured by his tone. After fondling her ear, to calm her further, he nodded for the handsome young daughter to lower the hinged side of the cage. That done, he motioned for the parents to crawl in, and then helped the daughter tie the cage closed.

Husband and wife both pressed their anguished faces to the plaited bars.

"How long, lord?" the man moaned.

Boy crouched beside the cage. "What do you say to this judgment? You are to be kept prisoner for the full passage of a moon, and to be beaten every night at moonrise."

The woman's face turned pale; the man gripped the bars more tightly.

"Aah, lord!" he sobbed. "We have spent our life walking free beneath the sky. Do not keep us here so long! I fear what will become of us!"

"What about the beatings? Do you fear those too?"

The man gazed at him tearfully, his eyes no longer ugly, but forlorn and pitiful. "We care nothing for the beatings, lord. But this prison! A month in here will drive us mad!"

Boy nodded to the daughter once more, for her to lower the hinged side of the cage and release them.

"Was this their punishment?" she asked in a puzzled voice. "This alone?"

"They have seen the world through their victim's eyes," he said. "That is punishment enough."

"How must I answer then?" she said doubtfully. "I, who tugged at your rope and tormented you?"

"You were a child," he said, and turned away. "There is nothing to answer."

But halfway down the hill, he heard quick footsteps behind him.

"I don't understand, lord," she pleaded. "Explain it to me."

He let her walk on with them, talking as he went. "When I was a child, I ate my meat raw. I wolfed it down like the dog who reared me. Does that mean I'm still a beast?"

"No, lord."

He paused on reaching the riverbed and looked deep into her face. He could see no sign of viciousness in her youthful features.

"Well, it's the same for you," he said slowly. "What we do and what we are … these two things aren't always the same." Before she could answer, he sniffed the air and pointed to a spot three paces away. "If you need water for the house, dig your next well there."

"You repay cruelty with kindness?" she called after him.

"We all have to pay in the end," he called back. "For everything, good or bad."

Magda, who had said nothing until then, moved up beside him as they journeyed on. Pulling something from her pocket, she held it out for him to see: a bear's tooth, threaded on a golden chain. It was the same tooth she had pressed into his punctured ear when he was a baby; and that he in turn had pressed into her hand on the day he left the village.

"This is my most precious possession," she said. "See how beautiful it is, and yet it was ripped from the mouth of a dying bear. Must that cruel act be paid for too?"

He waved vaguely toward the peaks, which loomed

nearer by the hour. "I expect so. The mountain will probably demand payment one day."

"We have both owned it," she pointed out. "So which of us will be called on to pay?"

"Both perhaps."

She stopped in mid-stride, her face dark with suppressed anger. "Haven't I paid enough?" she burst out passionately.

He gave her a questioning look. "How do you mean?"

But she had already said more than she had intended. Avoiding his eyes, she clicked her tongue for Girl and Faith to follow, and hurried away, eager to reach her village home.

19

They sighted the village late one morning. Even from a distance, Boy saw with dismay that his fame had spread this far up the valley, for the villagers had crowded onto the riverbed to greet him. Understandably, many appeared older, their bodies more bent. He had been prepared for that. What shocked him was how starved they looked, how gaunt and lean. The children were in the worst state: their bellies swollen; their eyes too large for their ravaged faces; their arms and legs stick-thin. Yet one and all, they knelt in the sand as he approached and touched their foreheads to the ground.

Faith, now a sturdy pup, romped among them, excited by so large a gathering, and Boy had to call her off.

"Why do you greet us like this?" he asked the people accusingly. "You know Magda of old. You have known me since my infancy. We're ordinary folk like you."

Phylo was the first to rise, the others following hesitantly.

"We were mistaken about you, lord," he said, "and for that we beg your ..."

"Lord?" Boy interrupted. "Did you call me lord?"

"Indeed I did, lord. We have learned to see you differently since ..."

Again, Boy broke in upon him. "Tell me, Phylo," he said, pointing to the largest of the charms he wore, "what do you call this?"

"A ... a skull."

"Yes, but not any skull. It belonged to the dog who reared me. Who let me suck from her body; who brought me meat from the mountain. With a foster mother like that, how can I be a lord to anyone?"

Phylo hung his head. "I cannot say."

"Yes, but I can," Bartiss added eagerly. "We all begin as lowly children. It is what we become that matters. And you ... you have become a great shaman. The greatest of your generation. I think I always knew it in my heart, but now I see the signs. I see them clearly."

"So what are these signs you failed to see earlier?"

"The ... the charms you wear," Bartiss began less confidently. "And ... and the set of your ... your face. I mean the way you ... you ..."

As he stuttered to a stop, Boy shook his head and smiled. "The truth, Bartiss, is this. You failed as a shaman, and so did I. My days of greatness are over."

Phylo gave him a look of consternation, as did many of the villagers.

"Does that mean you won't help us?" he said in an anguished voice. "Consider our dying crops. And our children. Our children especially!" He paused long enough to drag a leather purse from his belt. "We are not a rich people, as you well know, but what little we have is yours. We pledge it with free hearts."

Boy eyed the purse suspiciously. "What do you have there?"

Phylo upended it onto the sand, spilling out a small heap of gold trinkets, stored by the villagers over the generations. "It is not much, lord. As I say, we are ..."

"Yes, but what is it *for*?" Boy nearly shouted.

Phylo raised his eyebrows in surprise. "Why, payment

of course. For wells or rain or whatever you care to give. Travelers from Delta told us how you find water for gold, and we thought ... we thought ..."

He also stuttered to a halt as Boy strode forward, scooped up the trinkets, and crammed them back into the purse.

"Keep your payment," he said. "This is where I grew up. It's the one place on earth I can call home. If we need water, I'll do my best to find it, without reward. I'll do it for my own sake, and Magda's, as well as yours."

His words were greeted with sighs of relief and laughter. People came forward to stroke his cheeks and embrace him. Others greeted Magda with tearful smiles. While others again fondled Girl and admired her pup.

Still talking happily among themselves, they ushered the new arrivals up to the village and offered them the use of a freshly built hut.

"I thank you for your kindness," Magda said, addressing them all. "But if I am to stay here in the village, I will need more than shelter." She glanced meaningfully at Phylo and Nessa. "To eat, I will also need work."

"A good servant is always welcome," Nessa said graciously.

Phylo nodded his agreement. "We will take you back, and gladly."

Magda was about to go across and thank them when Boy stepped in her way. It wasn't something he had planned, or even thought about. There and then it just felt wrong for Magda to slip back into her old life, with nothing to show for the years in between.

"No!" he said decisively. "Your days as a servant are over."

"But I have to live somehow," she reasoned.

He moved back, as if to see her more clearly, and the sight of her white hair and aging features served to jog loose a memory of his last visit to the mansion. Reaching into the inner pocket of his tunic, he drew out the last of his wealth: the small sack of gold coins he had hidden there.

"Here," he said, pressing it into her hand, "buy land down near the river. If you must work, then work for yourself."

She gazed wonderingly at him. "Why are you doing this? Is it payment for my time as a servant in Delta?"

"If you like."

"But that was a gift."

"Then it's for what you did for me as a child."

"That was a gift too."

"So is this," he said, closing her fingers around the sack.

She did not laugh with joy, or even dissolve into tears, as he might have hoped. She merely frowned, like someone less than satisfied.

"I don't deserve this," she said in level tones. "I have been a bad woman and lived a bad life."

"Nonsense!" Phylo said loudly, saving the situation. "You were always the best of servants, and I'll see to it that you get the best possible land. The way you work, it will become a fine garden in no time."

There the matter ended for a while. Tired from her morning's walk, Magda went off to rest, but not Boy. Having eaten what little the village could offer, he walked down to inspect the riverbed—most of the villagers trooping after him.

He discovered only one working well, so deep that it had been lined with rocks and clay to prevent its sides caving in. As he was being lowered into it, he smelled the musty odor of stale water; and when he landed at the bottom, he stepped into a stagnant pool. Back on the surface again, he began combing the riverbed in search of surface streams. But this far upriver, so close to the source, there were none to be found. Through the many years of drought, the only fresh water had come from the heights each summer, when the sun melted snow from the peaks. These feeble trickles lingered in the sand, but they were deep down, close to the river's shaley bed, so it was hard for him to locate them.

He finally pinpointed three of these trickles, and straightaway the villagers set to work. He dug with them for the rest of the afternoon, and throughout the following day. Early in the evening they struck water. It was of good quality, though there was little of it. A bucket or two each hour was all they collected during the night—enough for the people to drink, but not nearly enough to revive their gardens.

So the next morning they began digging again, through a mixture of rock and sand this time. It was cruel, back-breaking labor, and after nearly a week it yielded the same result as before. Their third excavation was no more rewarding. Nor were the fourth and fifth wells, as Boy searched ever farther downriver.

After nearly a month of bruising labor, they were hardly better off than when they had started. Sitting wearily outside his hut in the cool of the evening, Boy was approached by Phylo.

"The people are too weak and hungry to go on like this," he said sadly.

Boy nodded his agreement. "What we need are shallower streams. For those, we'll probably have to go much farther, down to where the valley broadens."

Phylo pursed his lips doubtfully. "What good will they

do us down there? We're already exhausted. We could never carry water over that distance."

Boy knew that what Phylo said was true. "All right, we'll move the village," he said desperately. "We'll rebuild it wherever we find good water."

Phylo looked no less doubtful. "That will take us out of this part of the valley, where the soils are good. We'll be in stony, desert country, and only saltbush and cactus flourish there. In any case, with or without water, we lack the strength to rebuild an entire village."

While they had been talking, a small crowd had gathered. Many murmured their support for Phylo's last remarks.

"This is our own dear home," Nessa said. "An ancient and beloved place. For some, leaving it would be worse than famine or death."

Phylo's mother, old Sarah—bent nearly double now—pounded on the earth with her stick. "Aye, this is where our ancestors were born, and where I will rest my bones."

"Sarah's right," Bartiss said loudly, pushing his way to the front. "It's not a new village we need. Nor more empty wells. It's rain."

"Yes, rain," other voices sang out.

Someone brought a flaming torch and thrust it into Phylo's hand.

"Tell him," the same voices demanded.

"Yes, you're the village elder, tell him."

"Tell me what?" Boy asked.

Although it was now cool, Phylo paused to wipe the sweat from his brow. In the smoky light of the torch, he looked awkward and out of sorts.

"We have been talking among ourselves," he admitted to Boy. "The general feeling is that … that …" He coughed uncomfortably, "… that there isn't enough water left in the river. Not up here, close to the mountains. Rain is the one thing that can save us. We've tried praying to the Great Father, but ..."

"That we have," Sarah cried, speaking over him. "We've prayed these many long years, and where has it got us?"

Bartiss nudged Phylo, making the torch waver. "Get to the point," he muttered.

"Yes, the point ... the point ...," Phylo stammered. "Well, the point is this. The Great Father has closed His ears to our pleas. To make Him listen, we need a shaman. A great shaman ..." He took a slow breath. "Someone ... like ... like you," he finished lamely.

"No, not like me," Boy said with a shake of the head. "I can sniff out water, that's all, the same as a dog. I can't make the rain fall."

"Some of us think you can," Bartiss said stoutly. "I know I treated you poorly once, but I was wrong. I was as blind as everyone else. Well, it's different now. We can all see you as you are. As a rainmaker. The clouds will come if *you* call them. I should know. I've tried and failed."

"Yes, Bartiss knows what he's talking about," Phylo said more confidently. "If you went to the Great Father and pleaded our case, He'd listen. To *you* He would."

"Because you're not the same as other men," Phylo said eagerly, and began numbering Boy's qualities on his fingers. "You were born of the mountain; brought to us by the wild river; saved from the eagle and the bear; and ... and ... what else? Ah yes, you were kissed by the fire. All the great forces combined to create you. See ...," He pointed at Boy's charms. "You wear their emblems; you wield their power. You alone can make it rain. If the Great Father listens to anyone, it will be to you."

Boy held both hands up helplessly—though in fact,

191

Phylo's words had touched something inside him. They had sparked into life his dormant dreams. Perhaps he *could* make rain, he thought secretly. Perhaps he *was* of noble birth after all. Or at least a kind of noble birth—sired by the mountain and fashioned in the womb of the Earth Mother. Magda, for one, had called him the rainchild; and down the whole length of the river, people had greeted him as a shaman. Could they all be wrong? All of them?

As though guessing at Boy's innermost thoughts, Phylo pressed his advantage. "In the world of men, you are fatherless and motherless. Do you know of anybody else who can make such a claim? Also, why were you brought to us on a flood? Have you thought about that? It was surely another sign. A message from on high, that your life is linked to the life of the river. And to rain. Can't you see? You were *created* to help us; to break this drought that weighs upon the people so heavily. That is the purpose for which you were sent. For which you were made."

Almost persuaded, in spite of himself, Boy surveyed the ring of faces once more. How poor and downtrodden they appeared in the flickering torchlight, but how trusting. How confident of his mysterious powers. All but one were gazing at him with rapt attention. The only exception was Magda. She was frowning again, the way she had frowned when he'd handed her the gold. No, it was worse than that this time: she was staring at him with open disapproval.

"I thought you were the least of men," she muttered. "You told me so yourself."

"Don't listen to her," Nessa said angrily, pushing Magda away. "A scrap of land to call her own, and she thinks she knows better than the rest of us."

"Yes, what's this about the least of men?" Bartiss agreed, and shoved Magda farther back through the crowd. "Could the least of men sniff out wells? Could he become the talk of the entire valley? Or win the respect of everyone, young and old?"

Sarah beat her stick on the earth with an extra loud thump. "I remember it well, the way he was given to us. Thrown up onto the shore by the river, the Great Father's messenger."

"We almost turned him away," Phylo went on. "Think about that. We almost closed our doors to him. Many of us *wanted* to, so why didn't we? I'll tell you why: because the Great Father was guiding us too. He willed us to take in the foundling, though we had hardly enough food for ourselves. He was preparing us for the day when this ... this riverboy ... this ... this rainmaker would return to the mountain from which he came. To start the cycle of rain and flood all over again."

"True!" voices yelled in reply, more torches now illuminating the evening. "Phylo speaks true! The rainmaker has come! And soon will come the rain!"

Surrounded by so many flushed faces and insistent voices, Boy began to weaken. He felt his self-doubt wilting before their certainty. Who was he to question the wondrous nature of his birth? Weren't his mysterious beginnings and miraculous survival supposed to mean something? And what about his unique ability to detect the deepest streams? Didn't that also mean something? Didn't it point to some greater purpose that he had yet to fulfill?

"Rainmaker ... rainmaker ... rainmaker ...," the people began chanting.

Then, close to his ear, Phylo's familiar voice: "Will you plead our cause to the mountain? Will you?"

"I ... I ... I'll try," he heard himself say.

The chanting stopped instantly, the villagers falling

to their knees. In the awed silence that followed, someone laughed unhappily over near the outer edge of the crowd. But what was one dissenting voice among so many?

"Yes, I'll try," he said more firmly.

20

Boy left the village before first light. As he rose from his bed, he heard Magda stir on the far side of the hut.

"This is a mistake," she said, speaking softly through the early morning dark. "You shouldn't be going up there."

"Why not?"

"Because this is your old dream come back to life: the one that drove you to Arron's door. You think you can become a great shaman and conjure the clouds to open for you."

"Perhaps I can. I have conjured water from sand a thousand times over. This may not be so different. It may well be what I was born to do. What the Great Father created me for."

He heard her sigh impatiently. "What do you know of your birth? What does anyone in the village know? You came to us as a dogboy. A foundling. Be satisfied with that."

"I thought you said I was special," he reminded her, and hoisted to his shoulder the light pack he had prepared the night before.

"So you are. You began with nothing and have risen to a position of respect. That should be 'special' enough for anyone."

"Not for me," he said, and ducked out through the doorway.

"No, wait!" she called after him. "I'm not done. I have more to …"

Her voice faded into the surrounding silence as he picked his way between the huts. Girl and Faith both padded after him, but at the edge of the village, he turned and ordered them back.

"Go on now," he whispered. "This isn't a hunting trip. It's not for you. Nor for you, Faith," he added, as the pup crept forward to lick his hand. "This is a man's work, not a dog's."

They slunk away, disappointed, their tails between their legs, and he strode on alone, out into the dark.

By first light, he was well up the valley. And at midday he came upon the remains of a small settlement, wiped out by the drought. Had he but known it, this was the first shore he had been washed up on as an infant. Here, a woman had pleaded for his life. Later, she had crept down to the riverbank with a woven crib in which he had ridden the wild waters. Now, all that remained of those unknown days was a ruined hut—its roof fallen in, its walls crumbling—and a stone-lined well out on the riverbed.

He stopped there long enough to climb down into the well, which contained a small pool of seepage. Having slaked his thirst and refilled his bottle, he continued his journey.

It was a hard slog up to the headwaters of the river. He reached the source—a tiny spring—just as the light was failing. Barely a trickle emerged from the spring in these dry times, but he stooped and drank again, grateful for the water's sweetness. Then he ate a little cornbread, and prepared a bed of withered thyme for the night ahead.

Lying curled up on his fragrant mattress, with the watchful mountain at his back, he gazed down over the way he had come. Barely visible through the dusk, though again he didn't realize it, was the place of his birth: a dust-dry riverbank, some distance below. Earlier, unaware of the importance of the place, he had left his footprints in the dust, his mind focused on much grander beginnings. And it was those same dreams, of somehow being magically born of the mountain, that occupied him now, as he drifted off to sleep.

The dawn found him already up and on his way. Before the sun could rise above the surrounding peaks, he began climbing in earnest. His immediate destination was an ancient chapel, a sacred place tended by a monk. According to Phylo, the monk could point him to the holiest part of the mountain, where Boy could appeal directly to its abiding spirit—the Great Father Himself.

He spied the chapel late in the morning, more or less where Phylo had said it would be. A small, tumbledown building made of weathered stone, it sat perched on an out-crop of rock, well short of the snowline.

He approached it reverently. Yet when he pushed open its wooden door, the interior smelled only of filth and death. All that remained of the monk was his skeleton, which sat huddled in a grimy corner, still fully clothed in a woolen robe.

There was no question of digging a grave—the ground was too rocky. So Boy dragged the remains out onto the open hillside, robe and all, and heaped it with stones, building a crude cairn very like the one he had fashioned for his dog mother. That done, he resumed his climb, up toward the blue-white blanket of snow surrounding the peak.

He stopped for the night in a snow-filled dip between two bony crags and prepared his final camp. With nothing to burn, he could not light a fire, so he did the next best thing. To keep off the biting winds, he built protective banks of snow. Within this primitive shelter, he dug down to the bare rock and set out his charms: the skull, the stone, the feather, and the claw. He arranged them around an imagined circle; then wrapped himself in a rabbit-skin cloak and sat at the circle's center.

From there, he had an uninterrupted view of the high peak, which was perilously close now, and of the overarching heavens. As full night descended, the stars grew brighter—so hard and bright that they seemed to draw ever nearer—and with them came the cold. It seeped up from the rock and filled his bones; it was carried on the bitter wind that licked down over his protective wall and threatened to freeze his blood.

He tried not to think about how chilled he was. He thought instead of clouds, of warm rain drizzling from overcast skies, and he muttered prayers to the mountain beneath him. Yet try as he might, he could not concentrate his mind as he wished. As the night advanced, and the cold grew more intense, so his thoughts refused to do his bidding. They strayed back to his aching bones, and his icy hands and feet. Rather than pray to the Great Father, he found himself wishing for the comfort of fire and the soothing smell of hot goat's milk.

In the early hours, even these thoughts abandoned him. Drugged by the cold, he fell into a half-doze from which he might never have awoken ... but for the bear—an animal fresh from its winter hibernation and on the lookout for food.

Its growling voice was what roused him. Too stiff to move, he watched its hulking shape emerge from the night. With a single sweep of its paw, it crushed aside a portion of the snowbank, and then stooped to sniff at each of the charms. When it came to the claw, it reared up and roared to the skies.

Boy, directly beneath it, closed his eyes and waited.

There was a thud as its forepaws landed on either side of him; followed by the stench of its breath, the flutter of its whiskers upon his frozen cheeks. He opened frosted lashes and peered out—into two piggy eyes that peered back.

What did they see, those eyes? What manner of mind lay behind them? As a small child, confronted by a bear, he had not bothered his head with such questions. He had gurgled with welcoming laughter and held out his arms to the great beast. Now, there was no laughter in him. Petrified by fear and cold combined, he whimpered deep in his throat, like a lost child again. He had forgotten about the need for rain, and prayed only to be delivered from his terror.

As he whimpered and watched, the bear's nose touched his. It sniffed at him curiously, much as he had sniffed for water, far below, on the dry riverbed. Its tongue licked at his bare cheek, leaving the skin raw. One furry shoulder nudged his, knocking him sideways.

Did he pass out after that? He was never able to remember. Nor did he have any recollection of the bear moving on and sparing him. The next thing he knew, it was morning—a gray, unlovely dawn—and his whole being ached with cold.

He thought at first that he might have dreamed the whole episode with the bear; but when he clambered stiffly to his feet, there was the smashed snowbank, and out beyond his cleared campsite, a series of giant paw prints wound away across the mountain.

He saw it as a lucky escape more than a miracle, and spent the next hour thumping his arms and stamping his feet, in order to restore warmth to his freezing body.

The risen sun soon completed the task of warming him. Cheered by its brightness, he rebuilt the snowbank and resumed his vigil, determined to channel his appeal to the very heart of the mountain. This was but the first day of his devotions, he decided. If necessary he would sit here for three days and nights, never mind the cold, until the Great Father relented and sent rain.

All through the morning he prayed, as he had never prayed before. At noon, feeling dizzy from the sun's bright rays, he drank a little water from the bottle, and later sucked on a handful of snow. But as the day wore on, his mind began to wander again, for now it was the afternoon glare that afflicted him. Hour by hour he dozed and woke fitfully, and once he slumped down onto the rock. Ashamed of his weakness, he squinted up into the sun, searching vainly for signs of clouds. The sky remained as clear as ever, like a smooth bowl of washed blue, unblemished except for a single black dot high above.

What was it he could see up there? It seemed to grow bigger even as he watched. Could it possibly be something falling to earth? A message, perhaps ...?

He flinched away as it rushed nearer ... grew swept-back wings ... eyes, a beak ... outstretched talons ... A screaming cry rang across the mountain, and all at once the thing was upon him—a golden eagle! He felt its wings buffeting his head and shoulders; gasped with shock as its talons grazed his forehead, reopening the old wound; threw up his arms to prevent that cruel beak from gouging out his eyes.

Fending the bird off with one hand, he groped for his cloak and drew it over his head. Still the bird attacked, tearing out whole tufts of fur, slashing at the exposed leather. It was all he could do to hold on, the cloak being tugged this way and that.

Help me! he pleaded silently, forgetting yet again what he had come there to seek. For the moment, his precious safety was his only concern.

As suddenly as it had begun, the attack was over. Still huddled beneath his cloak, he heard the click of talons landing on the rock beside him, and after that, silence. What was the creature doing? Had Boy trespassed onto its territory perhaps? Was that the reason for this aggression? He would have liked to peek out but lacked the nerve. No, better to wait here until he heard the sound of beating wings and felt the breath of their departure.

There was no sign of the eagle when he emerged. Shading his eyes, Boy peered nervously skyward. He could just make it out: a black dot again, spiraling up into the blue. Tentatively, he probed at his gashed forehead, which felt wet to the touch. Blood! A scarlet streak of it when he wiped his hand on the snowbank. Obviously, this had been no dream either, but something all too real. As real as the lumbering presence of the bear the night before. Why, the bird had even attacked his charms, which lay scattered over the rock.

He began arranging them in a circle like before; except that when he came to the feather, it seemed softer, silkier than he remembered. In fact, now that he looked more carefully, there were *two* feathers: this newer one, and, half-buried in the snowbank, the more battered relic of his childhood.

He placed them side by side on the rock and looked at them. Why this second attack, and what did it mean? As a child, he had been eagle-sized prey. But now ...? He had heard somewhere that eagles in moult were more aggressive. *That* could explain both the attack itself and the second feather. Was there more to the incident than that? He shrugged, unsure. Whatever the meaning of it all, he had suffered only a minor wound and again been lucky.

Shaken, but otherwise not seriously hurt, he returned to his vigil, which proved a little easier as the sun dipped toward the peaks. The glittering light gave way to mauve-edged shadows and a cooling breeze. Minutes later, the sun plunged from view, and with the dusk, the cold returned.

Wrapped in his cloak, he prepared himself for the night ahead. A windless night of sharp frost that bit into his flesh more cruelly than any bear or eagle. Ice formed on his tangled hair; his eyes leaked tears that froze on his cheeks; a dusting of frost crystals formed around his mouth and nose, like the hoary growth of someone three times his age. Deep within himself, he began to feel hard and brittle, a mere stick of a man, frozen to the core, who must soon break.

He had no time for prayer. He needed all his vitality, all his mental strength, just to resist the cold and stay alive. High above, the spangled sky, as unforgiving as the icy air he breathed, remained cloudless—like another, darker realm of frost, littered with ice chips for stars.

Midnight came and went. Dazed by the raw chill, shivering uncontrollably, he watched as the glittering sky seemed to fall to earth. Stars glinted on his cloak; on his charms; on the surrounding snowfields. He could hear them muttering to each other, in voices that creaked and groaned with age. He could not understand the sounds they made, but he knew they meant him ill. So it came as no surprise, shortly before dawn, when the snowbank beside him moved.

More creaks and groans followed. Then a sudden jolt, and he was half buried in a welter of snow. His chilled limbs responded sluggishly. Like an old man, stiff in every joint, he staggered to his feet. Still the muttering continued, a low chorus of groaning voices that caused the entire snowfield, between him and the peak, to shudder visibly.

Almost too late he threw off the drugging effects of the cold. Fully alert, he realized what was happening. Those muffled creaks were the sounds of fracturing ice. He could see zigzag lines snaking through the densely packed snow farther up the slope. Another lurching movement, followed by an ear-splitting crack, and the whole hillside began sliding toward him.

He was given no chance to turn and run. In any case, he was too stiff. The best he could do was burrow under his cloak and let the snow sweep over him.

The worst of it passed with a roar louder than any bear could make.

"Begone!" it seemed to say.

I will! I will! he wanted to shout back, but there was too much noise for anyone to hear.

Huddled there, crushed by the weight above, he waited for the avalanche to pass overhead; for the roar to drop to a rumble, and finally die away altogether.

In the awful silence that followed, he tried to stand up, but couldn't. With difficulty, he moved one hand, and then the other. Slowly, painfully, he began to scratch at the hard-packed snow, struggling to clear a space in which he could breathe. Once free to fill his lungs, he found it easier to work, and ten minutes later he had enlarged the space to the point where he could move his body. Now, with the terrible weight lifted from him, he began the laborious process of burrowing back to the surface.

It took some time. The dawn had broken when he finally emerged. Exhausted by his labors, he rested for a while on the churned snow, allowing the newly risen sun to soothe his battered body. As from long habit, he felt for the charms around his neck … and remembered where he had left them. Without hesitation, he burrowed back down to the rock and groped around, locating them one by one.

It was not until he had returned to the surface that he wondered why he had bothered. For two things had now become clear. The first was that his charms possessed no power up here on the heights, where other forces entirely were at work. The second was that he wasn't welcome in this place. If he hadn't been so blinded by desire, he would have understood this earlier. The bear had surely been warning him to leave, but he had refused to listen. The eagle had tried to drive him off, and still he had remained. Roused to anger, the mountain itself had moved against him, threatening to crush out his life.

Well, he had deciphered their wordless message at last. Sitting there in the morning light, he saw the whole pattern of events as an utter rejection of all he stood for. His absurd hopes, his arrogant pride, and his dreams of greatness, all were fully revealed to him.

Other shamans might succeed where he had failed. Who could say? But where he was concerned, the Great Father stood aloof, deaf to his pleas. "Begone," the mountain had said, speaking through a wave of tumbling snow; and he obeyed without protest, though with a sadness that sat close to his heart.

Wearily, he retrieved his cloak, stuffed his battered charms into his pack and began the long descent. At the chapel, he broke his journey briefly, to stand at the monk's grave. Before, when he had buried the body, he had felt no sympathy for this unknown soul. Now, chastened by his own rejection, he was moved to pity. The filthy state of the chapel, its desolate atmosphere, the way the monk had crawled into a corner to die—these things spoke of disappointment and a wasted life. In all likelihood, the monk had also come to realize that he had been found unworthy; that his daily prayers fell on deaf ears.

As a sign of their sad brotherhood, Boy ferreted in the pack for a feather—the more recent of the two—and placed it at the head of the grave.

"For you," he said simply, and continued on his way.

That night he spent on a dusty riverbank. It was within a dozen paces of where he had been born. Like his infant self, he felt abandoned in this dark place and yearned for comfort. Alone with his sorrow, he drifted close to despair. Time and again, as a wedge of grief lodged in his throat, he had to fight off a temptation to weep for all that might have been, and for what he had come to.

Eventually, impatient with his own weakness, he brushed at his eyes and dislodged a single tear. It fell unnoticed into the dust, as he settled on his spread cloak and composed himself for sleep.

Equally unnoticed, far out in the darkness, the thunder-heads slowly gathered about the peaks.

21

The thunderheads continued to gather throughout the next day. With his back turned to the mountain, Boy remained unaware of them. His immediate goal was the village, though what he would do when he got there he had no idea.

He reached his goal in the middle of the afternoon. As he stumbled through the gap in the enclosing wall, the villagers saw from his expression that he had failed. Sharing his sorrow, they followed him to Phylo's hut where he sank wearily onto his hams, like a man near the end of his strength.

"The Great Father would not listen," he told Phylo. "He rejected me."

"What about the power of your charms?"

"They have no power," he said, and briefly he explained how the eagle, the bear, and finally the mountain itself had tried to drive him away.

Bartiss, never one to be excluded, came and placed a hand on his shoulder.

"I know well enough what it is to fail," he said in a choked whisper.

Old Sarah added her voice to his. "We have all failed the Great Father in one way or another. Why, otherwise, would he treat us so?"

The villagers nodded in ready agreement, some openly mourning their past wrongdoings.

"Aah, we all have much to answer for, if the truth be told," Nessa keened, joining in the general lament.

"Be quiet, woman!" Phylo said sternly. "Boy has done nothing wrong. He went to the mountain on our behalf. He did his best for us."

"Yes, but he was rejected," Nessa came back at him.

Phylo pulled at his lower lip, his old eyes screwed up in thought. "Not necessarily," he said, addressing his words more to Boy than to anyone else. "These visitations by the bear and the eagle, perhaps they were only meant to test his resolve. And likewise with the avalanche. The Great Father may well have been chastening him—on that point I agree. But rejecting him ...? No, perhaps not."

"How can you say that?" Nessa argued. "He was driven from the mountain. You heard him tell us so yourself."

"No, all I heard was how he chose to leave. True, he suffered an ordeal that would break most men, but he survived the tests. He rescued his charms. It was within his power to remain." He turned directly to Boy. "Similarly, it is still within your power to return to the mountain and continue your vigil."

"How can I return?" Boy answered in an exhausted voice. "I ran away. I gave up my right to be there."

Phylo squatted beside him on the hard ground. "You can reclaim that right," he insisted. "The Great Father understands human weakness. A faithful heart is what He admires. If you return, He will forgive you. He will recognize your right to be there and open His ears to your prayers."

Boy ran both hands distractedly through his hair. "But I'm not a shaman!" he wailed. "The bear and the eagle told me so. They didn't treat me as a brother. They made it plain that I have *no* right to approach the mountain. None!"

"You have!" Phylo cried with equal passion. "You carry the marks of the eagle and the bear upon you. Years ago, I saw with my own eyes how the bear's claw pierced your foot. How the eagle nearly carried you off. And consider this scabbed wound on your forehead. Think of the second feather the eagle left behind! Would he have given a part of himself to anyone less than a brother? Would the bear have spared anyone but an old friend? Theirs was a savage welcome, nothing less. Believe me, they await your return even now."

"But I'm so tired!" Boy complained in a small voice. "I've walked far ... I've heard the voice of the mountain ... and I can't ... can't ..."

"No one is asking you to return this instant," Phylo said more gently. "Rest awhile. Sleep the night through. Tomorrow, refreshed, you will see things differently."

"Yes, tomorrow ...," Boy said with a vague nod, "... better to decide then."

Sensing a weakness, however, Phylo would not leave the matter alone. "No, decide now, *before* you rest. That will guarantee sweet dreams. Because you will know in your heart that you are about to save the children all along the river."

Boy nodded more confidently. "Yes, the children ...," he muttered. "They deserve to ... to grow strong."

Phylo sidled closer, the whole village looking on breathlessly. "Tell me, do you ever dream of rain?"

"Sometimes."

"Well, that is the sure sign of a rainmaker." He appealed briefly to the villagers. "Isn't that so?"

"The surest sign there is," voices sang out.

"Add to your dream the fact that you are a child of the river," Phylo went on persuasively, "and you'll see that there is but one course for you to take. One path to follow. And it leads up to the heights."

Boy let out a long sigh, as if the last traces of resistance were leaving his body. "Yes, the heights ...," he agreed.

But Phylo was not done yet. "Remember this: that above all, you are born of the mountain. You have no father but the distant peak, which longs to see your face. You have no mother but the earth, which cries out for rain. You, the child of them both, can save the valley."

Boy stood up, suddenly resolute, his face flushed with a lingering flame of hope. "Yes, I am the child of them both," he said in a stronger voice. "No one can deny me that. Nor refuse me my birthright. I was born of the mountain on a night of rain, and the time has come to reclaim ..."

"Not true!" a voice rang out, and Magda pushed her way through the crowd.

He looked at her in astonishment. "Are you turning against me? After all we've been through together?"

"No, but I can't stand by and watch you do the wrong thing. Someone has to put a stop to your foolish dreams."

He glared at her accusingly. "I gave you gold to buy land. I fulfilled your dearest wish. Would you deny me mine?"

"Yes, if it's based on a lie. I've lived too long with lies. I'm done with them."

"What's this nonsense about lies?" Nessa broke in. "Until a few days ago, you were a humble servant. Try holding your tongue and leaving these matters to your betters."

Magda flinched under the attack, but held her ground. "The truth is the truth," she said stubbornly. "No words can change it."

Bartiss brought his face close to hers. "So what's this great truth you know of?" he sneered.

"I know that Boy wasn't born of the mountain."

"Come, come, Magda," Phylo interrupted more calmly. "How can you make this claim?"

There was a long pause, in which Magda pulled her hair across her face, as if hiding from the many watchful eyes.

"Because I was there," she managed in a muffled voice.

"There ...? There ...? What do you mean, woman?"

She let out a low moan of shame. "I gave birth to him myself, farther up the valley."

"You *what* ...?"

"He's my son."

"So you're his *mother*?"

She nodded, burying her face now in both hands.

There was a bewildered silence, the villagers looking on with dazed eyes.

And Boy, cold with shock and unable to speak until then, reached out and grabbed her by the shoulders, swinging her violently around. "You! My mother!" he shouted. "It's not true. It *can't* be! Not a common servant. Never!"

"Yes, a common servant," she murmured. "But your mother no less."

A choking sob forced itself from him as he accepted the truth of her words. "So you abandoned me!" he said, his face working uncontrollably. "You left me there in the care of a *dog*!"

"What else could I do?" she cried in reply. "I was unmarried! A single woman with no husband. The village would have cast us both out if I'd told them. And I didn't know about the dog, I swear! I offered you to the Great Father. I left you in His care. I swear that too."

Phylo gave an awkward cough. "So you are his birth mother," he said in an embarrassed voice. "I can accept that. But who then is his father? He was still sired by the mountain—that at least must be true. The Great Father placed him in your womb. Isn't that why you gave him back? Well, tell us, woman." He paused for an answer, and when he received none, he continued angrily: "Come! Speak! Tell us about the father and how the child came into being!"

Magda brushed the hair back from her face and turned toward the assembled throng, like someone about to relieve herself of a great burden. She even smiled slightly as she spoke.

"His … his father was a peddler."

"Joel?" This one word came from Boy, who was staring at her with a stunned expression, his lips trembling, his face deathly pale.

"Yes, Joel," she replied softly. "A vagabond who refused to marry me."

All at once people began shouting and waving their arms about, some angrily, some moved to mocking laughter. As the noise died down, Bartiss pointed a trembling finger at Magda.

"This slut has deceived us!" he told the throng. "She allowed us to believe that this *dogboy* was a wonder child. She was the one who argued for him to stay. *She* told us he was special!"

"Yes, take away her land and throw her out!" others cried.

"No, that would be too easy on her!" Nessa shrilled above the rest. "She must pay for what she's done. Leading us astray like this! Passing her brat off as a shaman. A great shaman no less! When all along he was a common foundling! The son of a slut and a no-good peddler! A nothing!"

"Yes, let her answer for that!" the voices shrilled back.

Rough hands snatched at her hair and grabbed at her arms; the milling crowd began dragging her toward the abandoned well in the river. It was only Phylo, hobbling in front of the crowd, who stopped them.

"Friends! Friends!" he cried. "Be reasonable. Think about what you're doing. Magda has paid for her sins already. Look at her face. See the guilt in her eyes, and the misery it has brought her. Is that not enough?"

The crowd moved back, shamefaced. Their raised voices fell to a murmur, which faded to silence.

And in the stillness that followed, they heard someone crying. Not the easy tears of a child who weeps most days of its life; but the hard, painful tears of a man unused to the act of weeping.

Slowly, the crowd turned back toward Phylo's hut. There, huddled close to the ground, was Boy, his face crumpled and lost, his body racked by sobs. He did not look up at them. He did not seem aware of their existence. He was like someone wandering in a darkened land, a place where sunlight and laughter could never reach.

To some extent, the villagers understood his grief. How he was crying for the death of his dreams and the end of his ambitions. For the bitter truth was this: he was less even than a dogboy. He was, after all, just an ordinary foundling; and his only skill—the finding of water—he had learned from a village hound.

Phylo and Magda went to him together. Tenderly, they led him back to his own hut, where he went on weeping for a life newly lost. Nothing they could say would console him. Plunged in misery, he gave vent to all his stifled longing, grieving throughout the afternoon and on into the night.

While up on the mountain, lightning flickered, the thunderheads gathered into a single dark mass, and it began to rain.

•

For three days he proved inconsolable, and throughout that time the storm raged. The river flooded, the rain fell in torrents, and the ground became sodden.

Never before had there been such rain—or so people claimed. At the height of the storm, green shoots began appearing on the hard-packed slopes above the village. Fresh buds swelled on trees and on bushes everyone had believed to be dead. Near the fringes of the flood, frogs struggled out of the mud to croak their love songs; and birds, not seen for many seasons, flew in from happier lands beyond the mountains.

Like the birds, the villagers braved the lashing rain and high winds. Glad to feel cool water on their faces, they worked in their gardens, planting out the seeds they had hoarded for so long. At night, they sat in their huts and sang, as contented as the frogs.

Even when the storm passed, the rain did not stop altogether. Like Boy's grief, it lingered on for a week or more, falling in a fine drizzle that coaxed the gardens back to life and soaked down to the very bedrock of the river.

After nearly two weeks, the sun finally reappeared.

On the first bright morning, a golden eagle was sighted high in the blue. Minutes later someone spotted a huge bear drinking from the river. These, according to Phylo, were signs, and at his suggestion, they went in procession to visit Boy.

They found him sitting in the sun outside his hut, with Magda at his side. Girl and Faith lay sprawled between them. Although Boy's face was still puffy from days of weeping, he looked calm, one hand gently fondling Faith's ear. He had taken to wearing his charms again, and he smiled at the villagers when they approached.

As usual, Phylo acted the part of spokesman. He had brought with him a twig of fresh blossom.

"We thank you, lord," he said, and placed the twig reverently at Boy's feet.

Boy clicked his tongue in gentle disapproval of the word *lord*, and gestured toward the blossom.

"Why have you brought me this?" he asked.

Bartiss eased his way to the forefront, unable to contain himself. "Because it's the only gift worthy of a shaman," he blurted out.

"Then I think you mistake me for someone better than I am," Boy told him.

"I think not, lord," Phylo said.